MW00748770

**Scot Gardner** lives near Yinnar, a little town in eastern Victoria, with his wife and three dryads. He works with young people who don't like school, and expectant fathers. He plays didjeridu, grows vegies and loves Dreamtime stories and pyrotechnics. *Burning Eddy* is his third novel.

*Also by Scot Gardner*

One Dead Seagull
White Ute Dreaming

# BURNING eddy

## SCOT GARDNER

**PAN**
**Pan Macmillan Australia**

Visit Scot's website at www.scotgardner.com,
or email him at scot@scotgardner.com.

First published 2003 in Pan by Pan Macmillan Australia Pty Limited
St Martins Tower, 31 Market Street, Sydney

Copyright © Karijan Enterprises 2003
Reprinted 2004
All rights reserved. No part of this book may be reproduced or transmitted in any
form or by any means, electronic or mechanical, including photocopying,
recording or by any information storage and retrieval system, without prior
permission in writing from the publisher.

National Library of Australia
Cataloguing-in-Publication data:

Gardner, Scot.
Burning Eddy.

ISBN 0 330 36401 4.

1. Boys – Victoria – Fiction. I. Title.

A823.4

Typeset in 11.5/15 pt Aldus Roman by Midland Typesetters
Printed in Australia by McPherson's Printing Group
Internal artwork by Shaun Gardner

The characters and events in this book are fictitious and any resemblance to real
persons, living or dead, is purely coincidental.

For Dinny

# Acknowledgements

We are not islands. This book holds spirit and stories from the following . . .

Pauleigh Gardiner, John Nieuwenhuizen, Peter Van Berkel, Shane Cloak, Robyn Gardner, Dinny Slot, Jay and Ag Curry, Liam Gardner, Pam Reynolds, Peter Counsel, Shaun Gardner, Jen, Belle and Bryce, Tony, Janine and Amanda Hanning, Susie Zent, Peter Adams, Vaughan Reimers, Tara Harle and the plants and animals that give meaning to this pantheistic life.

# one

# SPIDER

I fell in love with spiders quite young and quite by accident. I was in grade three at Watson Grace Primary School in Sydney's west. Grey shorts, white socks and runners that were never allowed inside. They lived on the sill outside the kitchen window otherwise they stunk my room out, so Mum said. And a sky-blue T-shirt that Mum had ornamented with my name across the front in sunflower-yellow fabric paint. She's got a photo of me wearing it somewhere; no doubt she'll get it out for my twenty-first birthday.

We lived right opposite the school and somehow I always managed to be the last one across the oval to assembly. My sister was five minutes early and I was five minutes late. Every day.

I remember hearing the music start — the same

1

Rocking Rex track every morning, 'Let's Get Moving'.
I heard it so many times I can still remember the words:

*The sun is up and there's*
*Brekky in my tum.*
*It's time to get moving,*
*Time to have some fun.*

*Get moving, get moving,*
*Let's move it right along.*
*Get moving, get moving,*
*Come on, sing along!*

I can't believe someone actually recorded that rubbish. Kat was telling me about an interview with Rocking Rex that she'd heard on the radio. She said Rocking Rex was a multimillionaire. There's no justice in the world.

I remember at the end of the song, the bell would chime and Mr Cummings would ask people to shush. He'd say people's names. Mostly Frank Schott's name. 'Frank. In line please.' 'Frank Schott, hands to yourself please.' 'Mr Schott! Go and wait for me in my office. Now!'

Frank was a handy distraction. He'd slink up the steps and push through the door behind Mr Cummings. Everyone watched him. They never saw me scurrying across the oval. They never heard my lunchbox — with two sultana sandwiches in it — thumping up and down in the pack on my back.

One morning I had a grass seed in my left shoe, on the tip of my big toe, but I was running too late to stop and get it out. I started limping. Step plod, step plod, step plod. It didn't help. I slipped my bag off my back and crouched down behind one of the telephone poles that marked the edge of the oval. I quickly kicked my runner off. No seed. I tapped the heel of my runner on the ground and to my absolute horror, a spider fell out. Not just any spider; a big, hairy, grey huntsman spider that — to me as a third grader — looked bigger than a dinner plate. It was groggy, probably doped up on sock gas, but it was still alive.

I squealed. I stood up and squealed again. The squeal went on forever and when I ran out of air I just kept squealing but no sound came out. Mrs Davies was walking up the embankment towards me, footfall after heavy footfall. She wouldn't run for anyone or anything. I turned, still screaming, with tears pouring from my eyes, and bolted for home. Step-plod, step-plod, step-plod.

'Daniel, wait! What's the matter?' Mrs Davies panted.

Then she squealed. I didn't look back. Step-plod, step-plod, step-plod.

Mum was finishing the breakfast dishes and saw me from the kitchen window. She slammed open the flywire door and scooped me into her arms.

'What is it, Daniel? What happened?'

'I . . . got . . . BLAAAAAH!' I wailed, and held my toe.

She ripped my sock off but couldn't see any bones poking out. No blood. 'Where? Where does it hurt? What happened?'

'I . . . got . . . BLAAAAAH!'

3

She carried me inside and sat me on the couch. Five minutes later, my wailing had faded to a sob. Mum still couldn't understand me. She looked at my toe.

'Mrs Fairbrother?' said someone at the front door.

'Yes? Hello.'

'Oh, you're here. Thank goodness. Is Daniel okay?' It was Mrs Davies, puffing and hacking.

'I don't know. What happened?'

The teacher came in, her face red and spotted with perspiration, the corners of her mouth white with spittle. She was carrying my bag and had my runner pinched between two fingers. 'I think Dan had a spider in his shoe. Big grey spider.'

Mum grabbed my chin with both hands and put her face close to mine, her eyes wide with panic. 'My lord. Were you bitten by a spider?'

I sobbed and nodded.

She looked at my toe again and could at last see marks — a constellation of puncture wounds. She phoned Poisons Information while Mrs Davies sat on the couch beside me. The couch creaked and the springs popped and twanged under the load.

'Are you okay, Daniel?' she asked with her hand on my shoulder.

I nodded and at exactly the same time the couch springs broke and Mrs Davies' bottom thudded to the floorboards. She shrieked and flapped like a walrus but she couldn't get up. I stood up and tried to help her. She was stuck.

My body started shaking from the ribs out. When the laugh eventually made it to my mouth, Mrs Davies frowned and struggled even harder, levering herself up on the armrest. The armrest splintered and she crunched heavily back onto the floor. The boards under my feet shook and I squealed with laughter until I had to sit down.

Poor Mrs Davies. I should have controlled myself — like Mum said later — but the truth is I wasn't really laughing at her. Well I was, but the reason I couldn't stop was because I had brushed with the meanest, ugliest, most fearsome creature in my neighborhood and survived. It had bitten me heaps of times and not only had I survived, it hadn't even hurt. A bee sting hurts more.

We shifted after that. Dad came home from work one night and instead of having tea, we started packing. We moved to another state, from the city to the bush — to Bellan in eastern Victoria. I moved to Henning Primary and met my best mate of all time, Chris Gemmel. Shifting was the best thing Dad had ever done for me, except maybe giving me the *Illustrated Guide to Australian Birds* for my eleventh birthday. I don't think Katrina felt the same way about it. She was in grade six at the time and she had so many friends — boyfriends even — and she was always out playing with them in the street until dark. She left them all behind when we shifted. Not many kids around after dark here. Not many kids around at all. Kat just sort of curled up. Stayed inside and listened to music.

We live on the Bellan road, which is forty-nine ks long. It weaves through the mountains like a serpent and crosses Ammets Creek twice. I don't go down the creek much anymore. The water and slippery rocks freak me out. We live in the third house. There are only three houses on the Bellan road. There were more in the olden days but bushfires, plantations and blackberries have swallowed them.

There are plenty of spiders here — three species of huntsman live on our place. Spiders are my friends. Instead of feeding my fear, being bitten on the toe gave me respect for them. Instead of squashing them, I began to watch them. Have them crawl on me. Keep them as pets. I found a book in the school library about American Indians and there was a cool section about the symbolic meaning of animals. I believe in that sort of stuff. Different animals mean different things. It didn't say that spiders were horrible and should be killed on sight. It said that the spider is the grandmother weaver; always patient and watchful, responsible for the construction and maintenance of the web of life. It said that we are frightened of spiders because they can bite us and cause paralysis. Understanding and respecting spiders would give us the courage not to be paralysed in frightening situations. Spider medicine.

Mum's spider medicine was to spray them with hair spray. When the hair spray set, the spider's hairy legs couldn't move. They'd eventually die from starvation. Totally sick. I gave Mum such a hard time about it that she eventually grew to respect my love of spiders. The man at Poisons Information had told her that there are very few Australian spiders that can cause more than discomfort. If it wasn't a notorious funnel-web — heavyset, black and shiny — or a white-tail or a redback, then she had little to worry about. Keep an eye on him, he said.

She progressed from spraying them with hair spray to a special sort of shout. 'Danyellllll!'

A shout I could recognise from one hundred metres away. A special sort of restrained terror in her voice let me know that there was a spider to be rescued.

Bellan is where my life really began. Mine began, and life as Katrina knew it ended.

two

# SNAKE

I started working when I was ten. The year Toby was
born. I'd always worked with Mum in the garden —
since I was in her tummy, so she says — but when I
was ten I started grubbing thistles for Graham and Tina.
They gave me three dollars a feedbag full. On a good day
I could earn nine dollars — great money when you're
ten. As I got older they got me going on ragwort, the
prettiest weed ever — sometimes taller than I was —
with nodding masses of golden flowers. Cows don't like
it and it takes over. Five dollars a bag. I could make
twenty dollars a day on ragwort when I was thirteen.
Then the thistles and ragwort ran out. It would take me
a full day to cover the sixty acres of steep pasture studded
with manna gums and I'd only scrounge up two bags of
weeds, so they started me on the blackberries behind the

house. Twenty dollars a trailer-load. That's where I met Cain and Abel.

Blackberry, like ragwort and thistles, is a noxious weed. Some bright spark introduced it from England ages ago and it's covered almost every unused patch of ground in Bellan. A blackbird poops out a seed it ate that morning and in a week or so the seed puts down roots in the loam. It sends up a shoot as tall as me that eventually falls over and where the tip touches the ground another plant grows. In a few years one little seed becomes a rambling thicket that spreads like cancer.

Blackberry has thorns. Brutal and remorseless barbs that can tear you to pieces and in the early days I would come home looking like I'd spent the day fighting feral cats. Feral cats often make homes in the blackberry as do rabbits and foxes and wombats and wrens and whipbirds, and the bizarre thing about that is that a fox's den can be right next to a rabbit-warren but the rabbits are safe because of the thicket. Feral cats can sleep just a few metres from a wren's nest and the wrens are completely safe. Blackberry fences the predators out.

Graham shoots rabbits, foxes and snakes. I've been out shooting with him heaps of times. He's a serious marksman. He motions with his hand for me to stop, shakes his long dark hair to one side and takes aim at something on the other side of the gully that I couldn't see even if I had binoculars. The .222 always makes me jump but Graham stays rock-steady, unlike his prey — a few final kicks and it's all over. Another head shot. Graham has been deaf since he was born, but my hearing is brilliant.

Tina doesn't like snakes. Neither does Graham. That's why they keep the shotgun. We can hear the retort from our place more than a k away — it echoes through the valley and every time Mum hears it she looks at me and smiles.

'Another snake,' she says.

Graham has a thing about hanging them on the front fence until they rot and fall apart. Bit disgusting.

On the third day of work on the blackberries behind Graham and Tina's place I had hacked my way into a small rocky clearing and stopped to get my breath, sweat dripping off me. A pair of scrub wrens darted through the thicket twittering and playing chasey — I couldn't work out if it was kiss chasey or British bulldog — and when their chatter vanished I could hear a dull scraping then a flop. Again, dull scraping then a hollow flop. Moving quietly into the clearing I spotted them — a pair of tiger snakes entwined in a love dance, pushing against each other, heads lifting off the ground, swaying then flopping onto the sunlit rock beneath them. Their movements were liquid and a pleasure to watch. I stood there mesmerised for half an hour. I named them Dave and Mabel. I wanted to run down the hill and tell someone but I knew Graham would get the shotty and increase his handicap by shooting two snakes with one cartridge. He can't see the beauty in snakes. Mum and Dad think the only good snake is a dead one. Kat says her skin crawls when I talk about them.

Later I found a great book about snakes at the school library that says it's normally two males that dance. They were probably fighting and the girl of their dreams wasn't far away, so Dave and Mabel became Cain and Abel. I told Kat about it on the bus and she told me to piss off. She's so rude when Mum's not around.

Toby likes snakes. My little brother is five years old. He goes to kinder two days a week. He gets a lift with Penny Lane, the lady from the other house on the Bellan road. She lives on one hundred and sixty wild acres of goats and blackberries. Her husband died three years ago when a tractor rolled on him. She looks at the ground when she talks. Her daughter Peta goes to kinder with Toby. They're best friends. So Toby pastes and paints for two days, and runs around home with hardly any clothes on the rest of the time. Mum gets paranoid in the spring when he's tearing around in the long grass, knowing that the Joe Blakes are waking from their winter slumber.

I found a tiger snake at the back of Dad's aviaries last summer. Dad keeps caged birds like parrots and doves, and the snake would have been after the mice that live under the feed bin. Kind of handy to have around. It was curled up when I found it, quite content inside a coil of black poly-pipe. The budgies were going berserk. I wanted to open their cage. I wanted to see them fly into the trees. I went back to grab Tobe and gave him a piggy-back up to the aviary, then sat him on my knee a safe distance from the snake. It had just shed its skin and it was glossy like wet paint. For the Indians, the shedding of skin symbolises death and rebirth.

Tobe's eyes nearly popped out of his head. His mouth dropped open and he pointed. 'Snate,' he whispered.

11

I nodded and the snake's tongue darted out. I put my finger to my lips and walked gently away, holding his hand.

'Beautiful, hey Tobe?'

Toby nodded with a big smile on his face.

'When you see a snake, go the other way. Okay?'

He nodded and thought for a minute. 'Walk or run?' he asked.

I chuckled. 'Walk or run. They can bite you but they are frightened of you. Walk is good. Run if you want.'

Two times last summer, Toby came up to me and pulled on the leg of my shorts.

'Snate,' he said, and proceeded to tiptoe through the yard to where he'd spotted a sleeping serpent. One turned out to be a piece of poly-pipe in the grass; the other was a tiger snake, up behind the aviaries again. It looked bigger and more vividly banded than the first time we'd seen it, if it was the same snake.

'We should give it a name, Dan,' he suggested.

'Yeah, good idea. What?'

'Zeb,' he said.

I looked at him. 'That's a good name, Tobe. Where did you get that from?'

He shrugged. 'I just made it up. Zeb . . . Zebbie . . . Zebra. From his stripes.'


Word about me working on blackberries got around. Tina and the mayor of Greater Carmine, Antonio Calais, are good mates. Mr Calais lives in a posh house in Henning, the township at the western end of the Bellan road where Kat and I catch the bus every morning. I started doing a couple of hours on his blackberries after school and a few weeks later he got me going on his ride-on mower, cleaning his pond, weeding the rosebeds, planting flower seedlings, and clearing more blackberries. He paid me five dollars an hour, cash in hand, and I worked hard for him. He told me about the Dutch lady. Said her name was Eddy. He gave me her address. He said he'd told her that I was good but expensive. He told me to go see her.

three

# YELLOW ROBIN

Tina drops Kat and me off at the bus stop every morning
on her way to work. She started providing that service
a few weeks after we shifted to Bellan. Every second
Thursday, Mum and Toby go shopping. They get a lift with
Tina into Carmine and shop and hang around town until
she knocks off work again. Tina's a scientist with the EPA
in Carmine. She makes sure all the power stations at
Carmine and Milara don't mess up the rivers and creeks
and the air. Big job.

    I went to the Dutch lady's place one shopping day.
Straight after school. I raced out after the bell and told Kat
that I wouldn't be catching the bus, that I'd get a lift with
Tina and Mum and Toby. She wanted to stay in town too
but we don't all fit in Tina's ute. Well, we do fit — but not
legally. Driving to the bus stop on shopping days, Mum

14

sits next to Tina, Toby sits on Kat's knee and I ride to the end of the dirt part of the Bellan road in the back of the ute. All the way to the tar. Like a kelpie. I love it. It's okay on the Bellan road but we'd get in serious trouble if we were caught.

No. 4 Concertina Drive. The number on the letterbox was obscured by vegetation. All the other houses, for as far as I could see, had a square of lawn and two shrubs. Four Concertina Drive was totally overgrown. A solid wall of greenery. There was no lawn, not a tuft of grass to be seen. The driveway was concrete but covered in fallen leaves. Trees had grown and met across the drive and I couldn't see the house. Ten steps along the drive and I still couldn't see the house. After pushing branches aside for what could have been a full minute, I found the residence. Well, cottage really, with smooth walls of earth and a chimney formed in blue-grey stone. It seemed to glow in the afternoon sun, filtering through the trees around it. I picked my way along a path to the leaf-laden front step. A small verandah protected a hairy old armchair. I rapped on the solid wooden door.

'*Ja*, coming!' sang a voice from inside. 'Just having a pee-pee. One minute, *hoor*.'

She told me she was having a pee then called me a whore. That couldn't be right. I jumbled the sounds I'd heard and tried to make sense of them. My head was still rattling as I heard footfalls on a timber floor. The door groaned on its hinges and an old woman peered at me with half a smile on her lips. She was short — probably no taller than my armpit — and she wiped her hands on

15

a blue and white checked apron. The shape of her face was familiar.

'Come in, darling. Come in, sit down,' she said, waving me inside.

'Hello, I'm Daniel Fairbrother. Mr Calais said . . .'

'*Ja*, I know, darling. And I am Eddy. Want a cup of coffee? Come, sit down.'

I moved past the old lady and into her lounge room. It was filled with fine leather furniture, potted plants and paintings — old sailing boats on high seas and one of a windmill that looked like a photograph. There was a TV in one corner and it was on but no sound came out. One of the guess-the-word game shows.

'Sit,' she insisted. 'Coffee?'

'No thank you,' I said as I sat on the edge of her leather sofa.

'Lemonade? Juice?'

I could see she wasn't going to be happy until I had something to drink. 'Water? Water would be nice.'

'*Ja*. Water is good. I collect my own,' she said, and vanished into another part of the cottage. She came back with two glasses of water and two strange-looking biscuits on a plate. She sat the plate close to me, took one of the biscuits and nestled into the armchair opposite the TV. Her chair was covered in a huge sheepskin rug. The old lady reclined a little and a footrest popped out. She sipped her water.

'So tell me, darling, you are a good worker?'

I shrugged and nodded sheepishly. If there's one thing I do well, it's work.

'Tonio says you have worked hard on his garden. You work hard for me too, *ja*? You work hard, I'll pay you well. If you don't work hard, I'll just pay you. *Geld verzoet de arbeid*. Money will make your work bearable. Okay?'

I nodded. 'What jobs do you have in mind?'

She chuckled. 'We can go outside and see. Finish your biscuit and your water.'

She reached over to the table beside her and pushed a button on the TV remote. I jumped when the sound burst from the speakers and somehow resisted the urge to cover my ears.

'Good show. I always learn something. My favourite,' she yelled, and screwed her face into a smile.

I picked up the lone biscuit from the plate and hesitantly pecked at the corner. A rush of cinnamon exploded in my mouth and before I could blink I'd eaten the whole thing. I finished my water and sat forward. The closing titles for her show flashed on the screen and she turned the TV off. She stood up and broke wind loudly. She took my glass and broke wind in time with her steps to the kitchen. I didn't know where to look.

When she returned, she was smiling. 'Did you hear that? I played a little tune with my bum! A *windje* song. Ha ha!'

She headed for the door. I held my breath and followed.

'It looks like a mess, *ja*? It is mine yungle. Mine paradise. When I shifted here . . . when my Kasper died, it was just grass. Now look at it. I am only growing plants that are useful. Some have fruits, some have a beautiful smell, some I can eat. All useful, *hoor*.'

I nodded. If I ever had to live in town, then my place would look like No. 4 Concertina Drive.

'It looks a mess but it's just wild. I am getting too old to tame it all. I tend my vegies. Here, look.'

She took my hand. Her skin was warm and soft and she led me to an open area planted with spring vegetables. It wasn't a big garden — the size of two car-park bays — but it was packed to the hilt with lush food plants. The fine leaves of carrots, a pyramid of stakes supporting beans with red flowers and long green pods, a neat row of cos lettuce and a border of what looked like garlic plants in full mauve flower. She took a hose and filled a concrete birdbath that was almost obscured by a citrus tree of some sort, and I noticed the birds. High in the branches were blackbirds, sparrows and a lone parrot quietly whistling and chattering to itself. On the ground, a wren family and a shrike-thrush were rifling through the leaf litter, hunting for dinner. It was an oasis for the birds of Carmine, I thought.

She instructed me on how she wanted things done. Not too much chop-chop — only clear the paths. Her tools were in the shed and the compost heap was beside it. 'If you run out of things to do, take the ladder and clean the gutters.'

She went inside. I went like crazy. I cut a hole in the fruit-laden shrub that covered the letterbox. The fruit were green and smelled like perfume — probably poisonous. I gingerly sawed a few low branches off the trees that hung over the paths, raked and then swept them clean. The walk from the drive to the front door was paved in red bricks. With the leaves and twigs that had covered it now back

18

under the trees, it looked like something out of a glossy garden magazine.

As I stood and admired my work, a yellow robin flitted out of the bushes and landed on the broom in my hand. To the bird, I was just another tree, the broom just another branch. It froze and watched the leaves I'd swept off the path. It seemed to fall from the broom onto the leaf litter, grab a white grub and then, in a sharp *brrrt* of wing beats, moved to a branch on an apricot tree. It beat the grub against the branch.

The old lady stood motionless on the front doorstep. There was a faint smile on her face.

'I . . . I have to get going,' I said.

She surveyed my work and nodded approvingly. She disappeared inside and returned a few minutes later with an envelope, which she handed to me.

'*Geld moet rollen,*' she mumbled. 'You can't take it with you . . .'

I stuffed the envelope into the pocket of my shorts.

She blinked and smiled. 'You have worked hard, Dan-ee-el, please come to me again. Clean the gutters. Come when you can.'

I wasn't at all certain about our arrangements for payment. On every other job, I had agreed on a price before I'd started work. I walked down the old lady's drive and along about four houses before I couldn't stand the suspense any longer. I ripped open the envelope and was delighted to see a red-orange twenty-dollar note. My mouth dropped when I pulled the money out and found that there were two twenties folded together. I looked at the envelope and with disbelief at the money, then turned to look at number four. The old lady was standing on the footpath watching me. She waved. I waved back and bowed a little.

# four
# WOMBAT

Our Leyland P76 was in the driveway, which excited Toby
and Toby alone. Dad was home. We unloaded the shopping
from the ute and Mum thanked Tina. Kat was in her room;
she would have got a lift with Graham. I could hear her
singing 'Waterloo', loud and out of tune — like she does
when Dad's home. When she has her headphones on. Toby
grabbed a bag of shopping that looked like it was heavier
than he was and struggled into the kitchen. Mum and I,
both hands full, carried the rest. Dad was at the kitchen
table reading a letter. Toby was telling him excitedly about
the new coin-operated digger at the plaza. Dad nodded and
kept reading. Mum said hello to him and he grumbled.
Toby tried to climb on him and Dad growled and told him
to get down.

'Come on, Tobe, let's go get the eggs,' I suggested.

'Ohh-kay,' Tobe huffed.

We walked through the vegie garden to the gate of the chook pen. The chooks had been out all day and they were flapping and beginning to roost in the half-light. I got six eggs from one nesting box. Toby got three from the other.

I held my hands low so he could see. 'How many eggs have I got?'

He was quiet as he counted. His lips moving, pointing at each egg with a nod of his head.

'Six,' he whispered triumphantly.

'Yes. How many have you got?'

'Three,' he said, and held them up.

'How many is that all together?'

He was silent again, head nodding. 'Seven.'

'No, try again.'

'Eight?'

'Nope.'

'Six?'

'No. You're guessing. Count them.'

He counted them again. 'Nine!'

'Well done.'

We started walking towards the house. Toby was looking at the lounge window with a frown on his face.

'Wanna go up the cubby, Dan?' he asked.

'We could do that, mate. For a little while before tea.'

We put the eggs in a carton and whispered to Mum that we were going up to the cubby. She nodded and whispered that she'd come and get us when tea was ready.

The first week that Dad had worked at the Milara

coalmine he'd brought home a huge packing crate on a borrowed trailer. He'd used it as his shed until he'd built something more substantial for himself, then I had inherited it. The crate doesn't have any windows and it only has one door but I ran a power lead from Dad's shed and set up a light and a radio. When Toby was three, I built a desk for him and a platform for myself so that we could still see each other, but he didn't have to be looking over my shoulder at what I was reading. Toby has his colouring books; I have my full-colour books locked in a small cupboard attached to the wall.

Toby wanted to paint so I brought up a cup of water and he sat and hummed as he slashed brush-loads of colour onto the page. I flicked through a magazine.

'Dan?'

'Yeah?'

'Why is Dad always so drumpy?'

'Grumpy? He works hard, Tobe. Gets tired.'

'Yeah, you work hard, too. You're not tranky all the time.'

'No, but some days I get cranky. So do you.'

'Yeah, but not all the time.'

'Yeah, not all the time.'

I heard the jangle of Dad's keys and folded my magazine. Toby must have heard him, too. He looked up from his painting and stared at the door of the cubby. I held my breath. *Knock, scuffle, knock* as Dad fumbled with the lock on his shed. Then *rasp-tink* as the key slid home and the lock opened. *Clunk* of the pad bolt. *Klomp, klomp* of his work boots on the wooden floor. *Scree;*

23

curtain closes. *Click*; light switch. I often hear in pictures. I heard all that and in my mind I saw a movie as clear as if I was watching him. Then another key rasped home and a lock clinked open. A drawer slid. Rustling papers. That's where the movie ended. That's where the movie always ended.

Dad has locks on everything. There's a lock on the P76's petrol cap. There's a lock on each of the four aviary doors and there's a lock on the liquor cupboard. If we had a phone, there'd be a lock on that, too. And there's a lock on the red tool box in the back of the car. The red tool box with the faded 'Steven Fairbrother' in black texta. All the keys live on his hip — a shining collection of brass and nickel that clips onto a belt loop and jangles whenever he moves. He should have been a security guard but he works in an open-cut coalmine. Twelve-hour shifts operating a conveyor. He's either working or tired from working so Mum, Kat and I have learnt to avoid him. Toby gets told off. Look out if the radio in the cubby is on when he gets home — he reckons he can't stand the noise. That's probably why we don't have a TV. Well, that and the fact that we could only get one channel, like Tina and Graham, and then only when it's not windy or raining.

I've never had a friend over to stay. Not that I have many friends who would want to visit but when I was in grade six at Henning Primary there was Chris. I visited his place and we caught skinks under the rocks beside the dam. Mum wouldn't let me invite him over. She said it wasn't worth it; it'd only make things worse with Dad. I wish I'd made more of a fuss.

Mum called Toby and me in. Dad said he'd eat his dinner in the shed.

'Come and eat with us, Steve. Please,' Mum said.

'Yeah, Dad. Have dinner with us,' Toby echoed.

There was a long silence. 'I said, I'll have my dinner in the shed.'

It's easier to eat when Dad's not around anyway. That night Mum and Kat joked, sticking their tongues out with mushed-up food on them and I played a game with Toby so he'd eat his dinner.

'Let me feel your ear muscle, Tobe,' I said.

Toby leaned forward and I tweaked his ear gently.

'Now, have a forkful of rice — no, two forkfuls — and let me feel your ear muscle again.'

He obligingly shoved two huge forkfuls of rice into his mouth and leaned forward expectantly.

I tweaked his ear again. 'Cor, that rice made your ear stronger.'

He grinned and chewed hard until his mouth was empty.

'Dan, Dan. Feel my eye muscle,' he said.

And the game went on until his plate was empty, then we headed off to our bedroom and rumbled on his bed until it was a total mess and we had to make it again before he got in. I read him a story and he nodded off soon after. Mum thanked me for that. I sat next to her on the couch and she rubbed my back. We heard Kat start to sort-of-sing 'Mamma Mia' from her bedroom and I looked at Mum.

She laughed. 'Kat sure knows how to torture a good song.'

I nodded. They were Mum's old tapes. Dad didn't like them.

'When we were in the cubby Tobe asked me why Dad was so drumpy all the time,' I said.

Mum sighed. 'Yeah? What did you tell him?'

'Told him he was tired.'

She grunted. 'Tired twenty-four hours a day, three hundred and seventy-two days a year.'

'Why doesn't he go to a doctor or something?'

'He's not interested in getting any help. Thinks he can sort it out himself.'

'I think we should bundle him up and take him to the vet.'

Mum laughed. 'Don't be horrible. Besides, who would drive?'

'I would. I reckon I could drive.'

'It's much harder than you think, Dan.'

'I'd give it a go,' I said, and something else occurred to me. 'We couldn't take him to the vet; they'd want to put him down. "I'm sorry, Mrs Fairbrother, he's got terminal cranky-pants."'

Mum slapped my back and we both heard a dull thump and a squeal. The house shuddered. We looked at each other. Kat was still singing away, oblivious. Thump, squeal, squeal. It sounded like a fox. It was coming from under the house.

I grabbed the torch and jogged to the side of the house where the stumps are longest. I peered under and scanned. Nothing. I stood and listened. Something heavy was moving through the grass beside me. I trained the torch on the sound in time to see a long, dark-furred, red-eyed beast hurtling towards me. I froze and it thundered past my leg and under the house. Thump, squeal, squeal. Silence. My heart raced and the skin on the back of my neck crawled as I flashed the torch under the house. I saw two sets of red eyes and I laughed like crazy when I recognised what it was.

'It's the wombats,' I shouted.

Mum laughed.

As I watched, the bigger, red-coloured wombat, Doug, bolted at the smaller, dark-haired Tilly. She took off and squealed — not loud, but like a fox or like Toby pretending to do skids with a toy car — before running headlong into one of the concrete stumps of the house. It rang like it had been hit with a hammer. She changed course and bolted into the paddock with the panting Doug in hot pursuit. A few minutes later, they were back again, running almost the same path as before. *Tooong*. Tilly head-butted a stump again. It's true that wombats aren't the smartest creatures on earth but they do have hard heads. That must be wombat medicine, I thought; be hard-headed.

# five

# SCORPION

I've always been deadly serious about school. Late but serious. When we lived in Sydney — grade three, maybe even grade two — I couldn't leave a class if I hadn't finished my work or understood the idea that was being put forward. Just made sense; we were there to learn. Frank Schott was the first in a long line of troublemaking idiots that I followed from class to class — and in the case of Michael Fisher, from school to school. He did grade six with me at Henning, then ended up in the same year-seven class at Carmine Secondary. Thankfully he was in 8D, I was in 8A, but in year nine he was back with a vengeance. He's not dumb and he even manages to get decent marks every now and then, but he always has to be the centre of attention. He's been going out with Amy what's-her-name since year seven and they can be quite pathetic on the bus — holding hands and kissy kissy as Amy gets off. I grunted once when Wayne the bus driver told her to get a move on. They couldn't bear to part and when I grunted she shot me daggers. Well, they were more like axes.

'Get a life, Fairy,' she growled.

Everyone laughed — including me — but the name stuck. Anyone with any respect calls me Daniel or Dan; everyone else calls me Fairy. Even Mr Reusch the PE teacher calls me Fairy. Chantelle Morrison is best mates with Amy but she calls me Dan.

I stuck my hand up in SOSE one day and Mrs Griffiths turned away just as I did.

'Mrs G! Fairy's got a question. Haven't you, Fairy?' Michael shouted from the back of the room. 'Shut up everyone, Fairy's trying to ask a question.'

The class went quiet and I looked over my shoulder at twenty-six pairs of eyes. Michael smiled and the gap in his front teeth made him look like a cartoon beaver.

'Yes, Daniel?'

I almost told her that it didn't matter but the laughter would have been too loud on my sensitive ears. 'If we have the technology to create solar power stations, why don't we make more of them?'

'Good question, Daniel. The sort that only you could ask,' Mrs Griffith began good-naturedly. 'It's to do with infrastructure. The power stations that burn coal — like those around us here — took a long time and a lot of money to complete. They employ a great many people — your father among them, yes? — and they'll be burning coal until they can't do it anymore. That is, when they run

29

out of usable coal or it becomes uneconomical to maintain them. Does that answer your question?'

I nodded but it sounded a bit stupid. Build a solar power station and you don't have to burn any coal. It's all for free. Didn't make much sense.

'Der, Fairy. If we didn't have the power stations we wouldn't be here,' Michael bellowed.

'That's enough, Michael, sit down please.'

At recess and lunch for as long as I've been at the school, I have played four square with Robert and Aiden and the two Davids. They're not exactly my friends — Aiden and one of the Davids are in year ten — but playing ball is what we do together. I'd say g'day if I saw them down the street but I wouldn't know if they've got brothers and sisters or anything. Aiden is the best four square player in the school. Sometimes the year elevens will offer a bit of a challenge but they're short-lived. Aiden's just too quick. Sometimes I'm number two in the school, other days I rank ninety-seventh. Totally rank.

I was thinking about solar power stations as I jogged to the old lady's place after school. I could see the chimneys and cooling towers of Hepworth A and B from near the water treatment plant. Can't wait till they run out of coal.

I rapped on the front door.

'Ja, come in Dan-ee-el. Have a sit in the lounge room, I'll be with you shortly.'

I opened the door quietly and perched on the edge of the leather lounge where I'd sat a fortnight before. She clunked and banged at the rear of the cottage for a while, humming unashamedly to herself, then she appeared in the doorway and I sucked in a startled breath. She had a towel wrapped around her head and another wrapped around her waist but her heavy breasts hung free. Her large pink-brown nipples pointed to the floor. I looked out the window.

'Ooops. Sorry,' she said, and chuckled. 'I am an old woman. My body has been with me for so long that I sometimes forget that I'm wearing it. Where is the cream? Ah!'

She walked half-naked across the room and squirted cream noisily into her hand from a pink bottle. She put it down and rubbed the cream on her face and neck.

'This morning I dreamt of you, now you are here. To clean my gutters?'

'Yep. I know where the ladder is. Might just get to it,' I said, and stood up.

'*Ja*, good boy. Before you go will you put some cream on my back?' She held the bottle out.

My face filled with blood and my mind filled with images from stories that I'd read. Stories safely under lock and key in the cubby. 'Old woman initiates boy into the joys of sex.' I wanted to run.

She chuckled. 'It's not sex, *hoor*.'

My neck prickled.

'Just cream on my back.'

I took the bottle and squirted cream onto my hand — it wouldn't stop shaking. I couldn't decide where to start. My hand moved over her shoulders without touching her. My heart was drumming away in my throat. The old lady sighed and my fingers finally landed between her shoulder

31

blades and spread the cream in an arc over her left shoulder. Her skin was as smooth as Toby's and lightly freckled. Her shoulders hunched a little and now that my eyes had recovered from the shock, I could see that she had a tattoo on the top of her left arm. A neat woven band that encircled her loose skin. The edges had blurred with time but it still looked fancy.

'My husband, Kasper, had a matching tattoo. We had them done when we were first married.'

How did she do that? It seemed to me then that no thought was safe from the old woman.

'There you are,' I said, and headed for the door.

'Thank you, darling,' she said, and undid the towel on her head. 'Be careful, *hoor*.'

'*Ja* . . . Yes. I mean yes.' And I'm not a whore.

I set up the ladder and cleaned the gutters. There were grasses and seedling trees growing above the back door, an apricot and something that looked like a tomato. I found a couple of black plastic pots and filled them with compost and leaf litter from the gutters, then poked the plants into them. An hour passed like a flock of ibis overhead and I whistled to myself as I packed up the ladder. I handed the old woman the potted plants. She wore a dress, an apron and a smile.

'Thank you, darling. Where did you get these?'

'From the gutter.'

'*Ja*? From the birds? Thank you. There is an apple tree in the backyard. Dead. Next time you come could you dig it out?'

I nodded.

She pulled an envelope from her apron pocket and handed it to me. 'Come again when you can, huh *schat*?'

She called me slut. Spat it like a curse. I couldn't believe that she'd called me slut. I only rubbed cream on her back.

'In Dutch it means "darling". *Mijn schat*, my darling,' she said, and laughed dryly to herself. I laughed with her.

'Ah, so you can laugh? Life is not so serious, Dan-ee-el. Laugh more. It suits you,' she said, and closed the door.

I looked at the envelope and then at the door. 'Thank you,' I shouted. 'Thank you, Eddy.'

The only reply was a crowd from the TV yelling 'Top dollar!'

On my way to Tina's work I opened the envelope. Fifty dollars. I walked on, whistling to myself and almost bumped into the mirror of a white car parked on the nature strip. 'For sale' it said in the window and a phone number. 'Mitsubishi Scorpion. 1980. One owner. With RWC $850.'

Mum and Toby were waiting at the front of the EPA building. Mum kissed me and Toby jumped up for a cuddle that turned into a wizzy-dizzy. On the way home, with Toby squirming on my lap, it occurred to me that I didn't have to limit myself to one day of work per fortnight at Eddy's place, so I arranged it with Tina.

'It's like I said to your mum, Dan. If you're waiting beside my car when I knock off work I'm only too happy to drop you home. For me it takes the edge off the guilt I feel driving all that way with just one person in the car. Any day of the week. You don't have to ask but I won't be waiting.'

I resolved then to go to Eddy's place the following Monday.

Dad was leaving for work as we pulled into the driveway. He waved out the window and yelled, 'See you in the morning.'

He smiled. Dad actually smiled. Not so I could see his teeth or anything but his lips curled up at the corners.

Mum looked at me wide-eyed, then thanked Tina for dropping us home.

Dad had mown the grass. In spring it grows so fast I can hear it getting taller. Well, almost. Kat was howling 'I do, I do, I do' along with the tape playing in her room. We dropped the shopping and retreated to the garden — Mum to pick some vegies for tea, and me and Tobe to make a fortress in the fresh-cut grass. Tobe insisted that we needed a log to rest our weapons on so I grabbed the biggest one I could handle off the wood heap and carried it over. The bark broke off when I dropped it and Toby picked it up.

'What's this, Dan?' he asked, holding out the piece of bark.

'Wow!' I said, and let the small dark-brown creature crawl from the bark onto my hand.

'Good find, Tobe.'

I held it low so he could see it. 'It's a scorpion,' I said.

'Cool. Can I have a hold?'

'Sure,' I said, and let the little beastie crawl from my hand to his. It flexed its tail over its rounded back and crawled across his hand. It tried to hide between his fingers.

'It tickles. Can they hurt you?' he asked.

'Not unless you accidentally squash them.'

'Then he would get you with his nippers.'

'No, his nippers are for holding food. He stings with his tail.'

Toby's eyes widened and he poked his bottom lip out. He encouraged the scorpion to crawl back onto my hand, eight legs moving in perfect time and pincers folded in front of his mouth. I wondered about scorpion medicine: always keep a sting in your tail.

'We've got to find a new home for him now, Dan. In the woodshed?'

'Yep, the woodshed.'

I dropped into bed at ten o'clock. I thought about Dad smiling as he'd left that night. I imagined him sitting at work. He'd be alone, I thought, sipping at the coffee that would keep him awake until his lunch at midnight. The roar of the machinery around him. I listened to the pair of koalas in the bush behind Dad's shed. I can still remember the first time I heard koalas call. I'd darted outside — must have been ten years old, it wasn't long after we moved up to Bellan — Kat was on the toilet and I'd desperately needed to wee. I stepped onto the evening-cool grass from the back door and, with a sigh, began to relieve myself. From the darkness came a low growl that grew into the most violent snorting pig sound. I shivered and managed to wee on my pyjama leg. I was frozen to the spot for a second as my mind drew a horror film of pictures. There was a blood-curdling squeal. The gurgling squeal of a child with its throat cut. In my mind, Toby — then not even a year old — was being torn apart by a wild boar. I ran to Mum, my pyjamas soaked and tears wetting my cheeks, screaming that Toby had been eaten by a pig. She bolted to the bedroom and found Toby sleeping peacefully. I couldn't believe my eyes. Must have been some other kid out there. She grabbed the torch and walked courageously outside.

'Mum! Don't go!' I hollered from the doorway.

She came back a few minutes later, smiling. 'Koalas, love, nothing to be frightened of.'

She had wanted to lead me up there and show me, put my mind at rest, but I wasn't going to step outside the door. She told me that it was a boy and girl koala. She thought they were in love. I wished they would kill each other quietly. It was more than a year later when I saw a big male koala, back arched, snorting through his bulbous nose in the middle of the day. At night, to the uninitiated, they are the sounds of monsters.

There was once a story going around at Henning Primary that Michael Fisher's dad saw a black panther in the bush in Bellan somewhere. His dad's an industrial chemist at one of the power stations. He's not dumb. Jack who has beef cattle up on the ridge in Bellan South says that he's had some cattle that have been mauled to death. Jack drinks a bit. I know Bellan better than most people. I've been camping on my own around here for nearly four years, every other weekend, and I've seen and heard some amazing things, but nothing like a panther. The sinister *chuck, chuck, chuck* of a brush-tailed possum. The kelpie with asthma that yelps from the tops of old gum trees, which is really a barking owl, and the haunting *whoo hoo* of the powerful owl — an owl as big as an eagle that eats gliders and possums. They're all part of the night and there's nothing out there that would hurt a person. I'm not frightened of the dark.

But that night, after the koalas stopped calling, I heard sounds that caught me off guard. Through the thin plaster wall I could hear Kat wriggling in her bed like she couldn't get comfortable. Of bedclothes being pulled aside but no feet across the floor. A throaty sigh, then another. Her bed banged against the wall.

'Unghh,' she whispered.

I sat up. I thought she was in pain.

More wriggling then a series of *plips* that I wished I'd never heard. I hid my head under the covers. There were pictures in my mind. Pictures that were not welcome. Sex pictures of my sick sister.

# six

# PANTHER

After school that Friday, I watched a group of motorbikes ride past the front gate. The riders carried packs and the five of them travelled in one long line to the bridge on Ammets Creek. I could hear them shouting through their helmets at one another though I only made out a few words. They were talking about the shack.

The shack was built before we moved to Bellan, probably a long time before. Poles of mountain ash support walls and a roof of corrugated iron. No door to swing open, just a hole in one wall. It has an earth floor and a chimney formed of bent iron that vents most of the smoke from the fireplace into the surrounding bush. The roof above the fire is soot black with initials scraped in it by wet fingers. My initials and others. It's far enough away from the gurgling Ammets Creek that I don't have water nightmares when I'm camping there, and about three ks from the bridge below our place. It was an exciting find when I was eleven and I've stayed in it quite a few times. One group of boys about my age use it and line the walls with their empty bottles of beer and whiskey. I've never been to the shack when they've been around, but I found a full can of VB there one Sunday and I thought about drinking it. I knew it would have been illegal and I thought I might have had trouble walking home afterwards so I didn't drink it. If I had found it on a Saturday, I might have drunk it.

They were heading for the shack and I smiled as I looked at the clear evening sky. A perfect night to play 'terrorise the tourist'.

I put Toby to bed just after sunset and Mum thanked me. I told her I was going camping and she said that was good. Told me to be careful. I slipped on my heavy cotton ex-army greatcoat and checked the pockets. Cigarette lighter, coil of fishing line, hook and sinker, knife and, in the breast pocket, a stash of muesli bars for emergencies. The moon was an hour or so off setting; a waxing three-quarter that lit up the track like daylight. I could see the shapes of wallabies feeding by the side of the road before they'd hear me and thunder off into the undergrowth. The air was still and high up on the ridge I could hear the mournful call of a boobook owl. *Mow poke . . . Mow poke . . .*

I made good time and could smell the smoke of a campfire and hear screeching, drunken laughter as the moon finally set. I guided myself into the clearing by following the rift that the track made in the canopy, stumbling occasionally, and came to rest in the long grass less than ten metres from where light and shadow poured out of the doorway of the shack.

'And the bit where he gets his tongue stuck on that . . . on that . . . chairlift thingy,' someone shouted.

They laughed.

'I think that's my favourite movie of all time.'

'Nah, mine's *The Wiggles*.'

Someone shrieked with laughter.

'Yeah, *Wiggly Wiggly Christmas*. I love it.'

'You're a wanker, Jimmy,' someone said, and punctuated it with an enormous burp.

Pigs. I knew who it would be, well a couple of them anyway. The burp would have been Michael Fisher and Jimmy the Wanker would be James Sheffield. I ferreted through the grass and found a palm-sized river rock and before I'd thought about it, I'd chucked it at the shack. Maybe I wanted to scare them? Maybe I wanted to sit with them? I didn't know why I'd done it but I chucked the rock and it thumped into the wall of the shack. The harsh clang was much louder than I'd intended and the sound rattled and echoed off the trees like a shotgun blast.

There was silence from inside. I lay down on my belly in the grass.

'What the bloody hell was that?'

There was a commotion, then a torch beam scanned the clearing. I froze and my heart made my eardrums boom.

'Down here, Fish,' someone said, and the torchlight flashed against the wall of the shack.

'It was a bloody rock.'

'Bullshit.'

'It was, look.'

Silence, then Michael Fisher growled, 'Whoever threw that rock had better piss off now or we're going to have to kill you.'

They chuckled and something moved in the grass between the shack and me. They grumbled amongst themselves then went back inside. I heaved a sigh of relief, smiled to myself and hunted for another stone. I wished I had brought a torch.

The sound of heavy padded footfalls. I froze again. Something big was moving between the shack and me. I could feel the vibrations through the moist loam, rattling my body. It was big. Big and heavy. My skin prickled and I stopped breathing. I fumbled for my cigarette lighter and dropped it in the grass. I went into a panic trying to find it.

'What was that?' someone whispered from the shack, and the silence that followed made my brain ring.

Panting, like a huge dog. Panting.

'It's nothing, Jimmy, you wanker.'

It was something all right.

The low rumbling growl made my whole body tighten. Then a snarl echoed around the clearing and I shrieked, still unable to move.

Someone banged the wall of the shack and yelled. Whatever it was padded to a halt next to my shoulder. I pulled my coat over my head and felt hot breath on my hands, sniffing at me. I tried to scream but my voice wouldn't work.

They were outside the shack. I could hear them through my coat.

'There, in the grass. What is it?'

Silence broken by my heart pounding in my eardrums.

'It's a bloody koala,' Fisher sang.

The beast near my head moved. It wasn't a bloody koala.

'Shit, what's that?'

Silence again and my hand started to shake.

'It's a friggin cow.'

It clicked together in my mind and I could see the movie clear as day. It wasn't a horror film; it was a documentary on koalas and cows. The cow, more likely a runaway steer from old Ted's, finds the koala moving along the ground between trees and sniffs around the little marsupial. The little marsupial, justifiably threatened by the imposing bovine, sits on its haunches and gives the steer what for. *Growl, growl* and a claw to the nose. The steer backs off and discovers another interesting thing; a human lying flat on the grass.

I sighed, but it was more like a moan of relief, and sat up. The cow crashed off towards the creek. Torchlight in my eyes.

'What the . . . it's Fairy. What are you doing?'

'Nothing . . . I just . . .'

'Throwing rocks at the shack, prick.'

'Yeah,' James said.

'Here, hold the torch. I'll get him.'

A new terror rocked my body. All the adrenaline generated in the previous three minutes kicked in and I sprang to my feet and ran up the track. There'd be no way any of them could catch me in the dark.

'Keep the torch on him.'

I felt like a rabbit in a spotlight, but the real panic didn't set in until I heard a motorbike start up. I hunted desperately in the fading beam of the torchlight for a way off the track but both sides were head-high walls of blackberries. The bouncing headlight of the motorbike replaced the steady beam of the torch. For a few moments, it lit the track well — blackberries and more blackberries — then the bike was alongside me. I ran as fast as my terror-powered legs would carry me. What now? Run me down? A hand closed in on the hood of my jacket, then whoever was on the back of the bike lunged onto me, sending me careening face-first into the track. My nose and cheek hit the ground and the darkness was lit by the stars behind my eyes. Whoever it was on my back got up. The bike stopped and turned. A boot crashed into my ribs, the blow softened by my coat, and another slammed into my lower back. The heel of a motorbike boot came down on the fingers of my left hand and crunched them into the gravel.

'Get a fucking life, Fairy.'

The motorbike creaked, then roared off, spraying my coat with little stones and dust.

I lay there for I don't know how long, my head spinning and the tearing pain finally filtering through from my hand. I sat up and realised I was crying. Gravel had stuck to my cheek and brushing it off hurt my hand and face. My fingers bent and straightened painfully but on command. Nothing was broken — except my will to live.

I hobbled along the track for what seemed like hours. The blow to my back had made my legs tingly-weak. In my dazed state I must have wandered onto an access track — one of the unkempt dirt roads that let vehicles into the plantations of pine, blue gum and mountain ash that line the Bellan valley. My boots made no sound on the track and, looking skyward, I could see the heavy angular shadows of mature pine trees. I stepped off the road onto a thick bed of pine needles and curled up into a ball.

I felt like my world had been cracked apart. I felt shattered, shaken to the core of my being. Destroyed. My hand, my face, my back, my feet, my heart — everything about me ached. I didn't have a life. No friends, a messed-up family, no hobbies, no sport, no interests. No life. They were right. There was nothing normal about me. I smelt the musty pine carpet below me and my waxy coat. Someone else's coat. Always someone else's clothes. I didn't even dress normal. I wasn't interested in girls, not real ones anyway. Wasn't interested in boys. We didn't have a TV. We didn't even have a phone. We must have been the only family in the western world that didn't have a phone. Why would we need one? You've got to have friends to make a phone worthwhile. Dad didn't have any friends, probably never has had. Mum wasn't allowed to have friends. That's what it felt like. Ran in the family this not having a life. Locked away from the world in our country home on the hill.

I dozed. My thoughts turned to mush. My back ached. I couldn't get comfortable. It started to rain as the sun was chasing the darkness out of the eastern sky. I dragged myself to my feet and walked home.

# seven

# FOX

We eat all our roosters. Dad can't handle the crowing so we cut their heads off as soon as they start. We dip the headless bodies in boiling water to make it easier to pull the feathers out. Sometimes the chooks go broody but we don't have fertile eggs. Mum bought a dozen from Graham and Tina to put under Henrietta and the morning I got back from the shack Toby was zinging. Eight had hatched and old Henny was proudly *chuck, chuck, chuck*ing around the yard with a swarm of downy black dots streaming behind her. *Peep, peep, peep.* I put my coat in my room and wandered into the pen. Toby caught one of the chicks deftly and held it to his face.

'Chickies, Dan. Aren't they gorgeous?' he said. A look of panic washed over him and he stepped back. 'What happened to your face?'

Mum did a double take. 'My God, what happened?'

She jogged the few steps to me and cradled my chin in her hands. 'Daniel, what happened?'

I pushed her hands away and spoke to Toby. 'Had a bit of an accident. Fell down went boom in the dark.'

Toby chuckled and went back to kissing his chick. Mum grabbed my hand and led me inside. She bathed my cuts and insisted on knowing all the details. I told her I'd fallen down a rock ledge, which put her mind at ease but made me swallow hard. My hand and cheek had swollen during the night and my eye was pushed half closed. My fingers felt as tight as a drum and no longer bent freely. Mum offered to wash and cut my hair while we were in the bathroom. I took her up on the offer. The feel of the clippers on my head was like medicine. Mum cuts my hair to a number three every month or so. Low-maintenance hairstyle. I don't have to use a brush.

I sat with Toby in the vegie garden that afternoon. Mum had collected Henny and the chicks and transferred them into a little cage where we could keep an eye on them. The end of the cage was propped on a brick so they could scratch around in the garden — a rare privilege for our chooks. They make a huge mess in the vegies — digging great holes in the beds and covering the seedlings. We fenced them out years ago. Toby kept both eyes and both hands on the chicks. He gave them all names and tried to remember which one he was cuddling. They'd flap out of his fingers and he'd chase them around the garden squealing, 'Hey, you cheeky thing. Come back!'

Dad was still on nights so dinner was a riot. Halfway

through our meal Kat froze. She had a huge forkful of noodles between her bowl and her mouth. She looked at me.

'What happened to your face, Dan?'

Mum guffawed. 'Oh, Kat, don't tell me you've only just noticed.'

Toby pulled on her sleeve. 'Are you blind, Katty? Ha ha. Blind cat! We've got a blind cat.'

Mum had just filled her mouth and Toby's stupid joke nearly made her cough it out. That got us all going.

'Mum cut me while she was doing my hair,' I said, straight-faced.

Kat looked at me and chewed hard. 'Bull,' she said.

I shrugged.

She put her fork down and squinted at Mum. 'Did you really?' she asked.

Mum laughed. Toby squealed.

My sister lives in her own little world. A place where *Dolly* is the newspaper and Abba is the religion.


After tea, I fought Toby with my good hand and we rolled on my bed until his hair stuck to his forehead and he couldn't stop laughing. He couldn't stop and I couldn't start. I couldn't sleep. Couldn't get comfortable and in my mind the movie played over and over until I sat up. I wished I'd had the courage to stand there. To fight or talk my way out of it. No, not fight. That would have been senseless, besides there were five of them and one of me. I wished I hadn't thrown the rock. I wished I could have walked up and knocked on the wall of the shack.

I lay down and stared at the roof. The moonlight reflected off Dad's shed window and through the glass behind my head, making Toby's old mobiles cast creepy shadows across the wall. A fox yelped quite close by. I uncovered my ears and listened until my brain was ringing. *Yelp, squeal, yelp.* Very close. I heard the dull *plunk* of wire under strain and my heart began to race. The fox was going for the chicks.

I grabbed the torch and hurried out the back door and around to the garden, the skin on my back crawling. The moon lit the ground and house like a distant floodlight. I could see colour in the blue plastic that Mum had draped over the end of the little chicken run. She had taken the brick out and let the cage rest safely on the ground. No fox. I scanned the vegie beds with the torch. Nothing.

I turned to go inside and the night air filled with commotion — yelping and buckling wire. I spun, torch ablaze, to see the little chicken's cage jumping and rattling. The fox was trapped inside.

With the hair prickling on my neck and arms, I crept to the cage and lit up the wire with the torch. The young fox was glistening with dew, motionless except for its heaving flanks. Beneath its paw lay the headless body of Henrietta, still twitching. I could see the leg of one the chicks: grey, lifeless and pointing skyward.

The fox stared at me, mouth open in a quiet pant. God, what was I supposed to do now? I didn't have a gun. I wished I had a gun. Could get Graham's gun. Just one crack echoing around the valley. One shot that would make Toby jump in his sleep and it would all be over. Thief. Murderer.

Thrill-killer with shining teeth. I thought that I could sharpen a stick. A knife. The axe. With a gun, the bullet does the killing. Quick. Clean. Anything else would be brutal and bloody. The fox was shaking. I sighed.

When I looked into those golden eyes — really looked — I saw all the knowing of a person. There was feeling in there. All the stories about smart foxes must have been true. It wasn't a dog in there; it was a person stuck in a dog's body. A wise person. An old person. The dog's eyes looked like the eyes of the old woman. They were Eddy's eyes.

I thought I'd leave it there until Dad got home. Let him deal with it. Let him work it out. Let him be the man around the house for once. I almost laughed — he wouldn't know what to do. He'd grunt and vanish into his shed.

Those eyes. Those golden all-knowing eyes, they stared at me with no fear. I could smell the waxy stink of fox, that heady scent of urine that hangs in the air along so many bush trails. The unmistakable smell that makes me stop in my tracks and look around. Somewhere, not far away, there'd be a scruff of red and blue rosella feathers or a hole in the bottom of a blackberry thicket that's just the right size, and the barbs around the opening would be tufted with russet hair.

I lifted the end of the cage and watched the shadow of the fox tear through the vegies and spring over the fence. At the edge of the drive it turned, eyes shining green in the torchlight.

'Go,' I whispered. Leave me some of your speed and cunning. Leave me some fox medicine. 'Don't come back.'

I heard a solitary *peep* at my feet and shone the torch. Little eyes fixed me with the part-lidded stare of death. Henny's body was still. What a waste. I counted the chicks. One, two, three lifeless little bodies. More. It was a massacre. There was another *peep*, and a black tuft darted from the cage and vanished into the carrots. I scanned with the torch and called gently. The torch beam shook. I couldn't find it. I doubted it would survive the shock and cold with no mother to hide under. The rest were dead. I left the cage propped on the brick and went shivering to bed wondering how I'd break the news to my little brother.

# eight

# CAT

Toby was awake when Katrina and I were about to leave for the bus. He's usually still asleep. I whispered to Mum about the dead chickens and she sighed with both hands on the sink. She apologised. She said she'd forgotten to close their little cage. She hadn't heard a thing. I took Toby out and showed him the chicks.

He didn't cry. He poked at one with his bare toe. 'That's a bummer, isn't it, Dan? Poor chickies.'

We dug a hole at the edge of the vegie garden and buried the headless body of Henrietta and the stiff corpses of the chicks.

'There were only seven, Dan.'

He was right. I remembered the one that had torn off into the vegies.

'Did the fox eat one?'

'Mmm. I think so, Tobe.'

He was still picking around in the vegie garden when Kat and I left for the bus. As we got to the road, I heard him squeal.

'There's one still alive, Dan! I found a live chickie!'

I shouted that he should take it inside to Mum and he whooped and called out to her. Lucky chick.

Dad waved as he drove past us on the road between Tina's and our place. He waved like he didn't really know us. He waved with one finger off the steering wheel like everyone who lives in the bush does. I waved back with my bruised hand. It didn't look like he noticed the gravel rash on my face. The skin on my cheek and nose had gone scabby and dark. My eye was mostly open and the bottom lid had gone the colour of ripe blackberries.

Tina didn't ask me about it until we were halfway to the bus stop, and I told her the story I'd told Mum. Fell down a rock ledge. She sucked air through her teeth. Kat said I'd cut myself shaving and Tina laughed. It wasn't until I was sitting in the bus shelter — with its graffitied walls and stink of piddle — that I realised how stupid it had been making up a story. In about three minutes I was going to get on the bus and Michael Fisher would look at me and howl with laughter so that I could see his gappy teeth and the little punching bag that hangs down at the back of his throat. Then he'd tell everyone what really happened — at the top of his voice — and good old Fairy would be the butt of everyone's jokes for another month. They wouldn't miss me if I didn't show. I got up to walk home and the bus rumbled over Ammets Creek Bridge. I realised that I'd have to run to miss it and that seemed like too much effort. Too much effort and then I'd miss school. I held my breath and stepped onto the bus as twenty pairs of eyes looked at my face. Some — like Ben, a little year-seven kid — stared, open-mouthed. Some looked on with mild interest, some glanced and looked away again. Michael wasn't on the bus. I smiled to myself and my face cracked and hurt. Michael wasn't on the bus.

Michael wasn't at school either, and when Aiden, Robert and the Davids caught up with me at the four square court I found myself telling them the truth. Telling them how I'd thrown the stone at the shack and how the pigs had chased me down on a motorbike.

'Well, Dan, I think that earns you an A-plus for bravery and an A-double-plus for stupidity,' Robert said.

We laughed and then played. It hurt my hand to slam so I had to play smart.


Amy what's-her-name stopped at my table as she came in for English after lunch.

'What happened to your face, Fairy?'

I shrugged. 'Cut myself shaving.'

She grunted. 'You're such a friggin' loser.'

I smiled and swallowed hard. I thought she might have been right. I collected my books and walked out. Walked out of the school and into the rain. My heart beat in my neck and my guts ached. I couldn't breathe properly. My lungs wouldn't fill. I walked, with rain tickling behind my ears, to Eddy's place.

There were two cars parked at No. 4 Concertina Drive. An old blue Holden wagon in showroom condition sat on the nature strip. A neat white Toyota sedan was parked awkwardly in the driveway, water beading on the bonnet. I walked past it and up to the front door. Bursts of laughter leaked through the closed windows and door. I couldn't knock. I wasn't there to meet Eddy's friends. I thought about getting to work on the apple tree but all the life had leaked out of my wet body. I shivered and sat in the old armchair on the small front verandah. I picked at the soggy scabs on my cheek until they hurt. They were still a bit fresh and I managed to draw blood. I heard a cat mew. A tiny, high-pitched meow beside the front step. From under the apricot tree crept a full-grown cat, a ginger tom with teeth flashing as it stared at me and meowed again. It didn't have a tail. The poor thing was half-drowned and I called it and patted my thigh. It sat down in the rain and meowed its pathetic meow. Someone inside coughed and the cat started. With renewed confidence it jumped onto the verandah and shook itself. It smelled my boot, then sat and licked the back of its paw, ears flicking at the bursts of noise from inside. I spoke to the cat gently and it eventually sniffed at my hand, then climbed onto the arm of the chair. It let me pat it — well, wipe the rain down its back, anyway. It tentatively stepped onto my lap and began purring like a not-so-distant helicopter. It vibrated on my knee for a while, then curled into a ball. My hand was covered in wet cat hair and I wiped it on the side of the old chair. The chair was covered in ginger fluff. It was Eddy's cat and I was sitting in its chair. It didn't seem to mind.

I had started to warm up again and think about what Amy had said. It made me feel like I'd eaten too many plums. It was quiet inside the cottage and I looked up, wondering what they were doing. Four pairs of eyes stared at me smiling from the front window. I waved, felt my face get hot and smiled back. One turned inside and said something in Dutch. Eddy came to the window, pulled off a pair of narrow glasses and beamed.

'Oh my Got,' she said through the window. 'It's Dan-ee-el. Hello, my sweet.'

She waved and the cat looked up. I waved back and the cat darted off my lap and behind the apricot tree. Eddy was gagging and spitting in Dutch to her friends. She opened the door.

'Come in, darling. Why are you here in the rain?'

I shrugged. 'Came down to pull out that apple tree for you.'

'*Ja*, but it is raining. You can't work in the rain.'

I shrugged again and stepped inside. 'I don't mind the rain.'

Eddy grunted. She turned to the linen closet and grabbed a clean old towel for me.

'What happened to your face, *schat*?' she whispered.

'It's a long story,' I mumbled.

'*Ja*?'

'I'll tell you later.'

She nodded, led me into the lounge room and introduced me with a wave of her hand. 'Luke, Annika, Claar and Tedi. This is my friend Dan-ee-el.'

Luke shook my hand, his long fingers almost touching

56

his thumb around the back of my hand. The ladies nodded.

'The nature boy,' Claar said, smiling.

They laughed.

'Nature boy?' I asked.

'*Ja*,' Luke began. He was a tall man with a scruff of thick grey hair. 'Eddy has never been able to pat the cat. Her Timmy. He always runs away.'

'True!' cooed Eddy. 'He is stray. For two years he has been living under the house. Sometimes sleeps in the chair. I feed him but I have never been able to touch him. Always so frightened.'

Eddy spoke to her friends in Dutch. I listened hard. I couldn't understand a word she was saying but I knew she was talking about me.

Luke raised his eyebrows. '*Ja*, real nature boy.'

Annika's hair was dyed flame orange and her nails were painted the same colour. She looked me up and down. 'Now we must be going. Nice to meet you, Daniel.'

They nodded their goodbyes and hugged Eddy before scuttling into the rain. The three ladies hurried into the white Toyota with Claar behind the wheel. Luke went to the Holden. I thought he'd probably had it since new. He let it idle on the nature strip for a full minute before taking off.

Eddy ushered me into the lounge room and closed the door. 'Your face, darling. Who did this to you?'

She sat in her lamb's wool and looked at me with her eyes pinched.

'Bit of an accident really.'

'Bah,' she said, and flicked her hand at me. 'Your face is scratched but your heart is bleeding, Dan-ee-el. What happened?'

The way she just looked right through me, through my thoughts, made me feel as though it would have been pointless to try to keep anything from her. That, and the feeling that I wanted to tell her everything. I stumbled with my words. God, I always stumble with my words. I couldn't work out where to start.

'From the beginning, Dan-ee-el. Start at the beginning.'

'There's this kid I go to school with . . .'

'*Ja*, what is his name?'

And I told her the story of my game of 'terrorise the tourist' that went bad. Of getting my face mashed into the gravel.

She held her hand to her mouth. 'Have you phoned the police?'

'No, it was nothing really. Something that I asked for, in a way.'

She was quiet for a full minute. Her eyes were locked on mine, sea blue and unforgiving. 'No one asks to be hurt like that, Dan-ee-el.'

'I really have to sort it out myself.'

'What? To be more hurt?'

I shrugged. I felt like smacking Michael in the head with a shovel. He'd have to be quick to hurt me again. I wouldn't run the next time.

'In Dutch we say, *je kunt geen vuur met vuur bestrijden*. It means you can't fight fire with fire. Always there will be someone ready to hurt you or steal from you or rip you off. That doesn't mean you have to do the same. Sometimes you have to close the door on all the muck.'

I nodded and fantasised about meeting Michael in the bush. In the dark. A car *shhh*ed past outside on the wet street. Timmy the stray meowed his pathetic meow.

Eddy smiled. 'You know, to see you with Timmy just now was a miracle. You can not *believe* how timid he is. When I open the door he is already under the house. How did you do it?'

I shrugged. Maybe I'm part cat. 'Just called him.'

'*Ja*. You really are the nature boy. Do you love animals? Of course you do. Animals know that. They can sense it. Feel it. Like the bird. When you were here the first time I saw a bird . . . little yellow bird . . . land on the broom in your hand. Just like you were a tree, but they know. They know you are friendly. They can feel the love.'

I looked at her and she looked out the front window. Her eyes lost focus.

'Like my dog, Ziggy,' she began. 'Ziggy was a sausage dog. With little legs and big ears. We lived on a farm at Bellan. You know Bellan?'

I nodded. '*Ja*. I mean yes. We live in Bellan.'

'*Jaaa*? Of course . . . near Tonio. Anyway, Kasper worked at Hepworth and he left early. One morning it got to maybe ten o'clock and I couldn't find Ziggy. He was always with me. Always. And if I was inside he would wait on the mat until I came out. So, when I couldn't find him I got worried and I started to call, "Ziggy, Ziggy. Here boy." Nothing. Not . . . a . . . thing. There were foxes everywhere out there and Kasper decided to set some traps

59

after a fox killed one of his beautiful peacocks. Killed her in the nest.

'I don't like traps. They are horrible mean things and I thought maybe Ziggy got, you know, caught in the trap. So I looked around the fence where there were traps and *ja*, there was Ziggy. My poor beautiful dog with his leg caught in a trap. His front leg. He was biting at the trap and crying.'

Eddy's eyes glistened and she swallowed. I wriggled in my seat.

'I didn't know what to do, *hoor*. I had not the strength in me to open the trap — it is hard for a man, impossible for an old woman. All the blood. Kasper would never be back until maybe five o'clock and by then poor Ziggy would be dead.

'And then there was a miracle. I prayed to Got, "Got, what can I do?" and the trap . . . I pushed the trap with my hands and it opened like a book. Like a book, and Ziggy, he scrambled away into the bushes. When I found him he was laying on his side and panting *huh-a-huh* with his eyes wide open, and I could see white bones poking out of his leg and I think that he is sure to die. I have not a licence to drive a car and it is so far to town. I could hardly lift him. I couldn't carry him. Ziggy looked up at me and I prayed to Got again, "Got, help my Ziggy," and I put my hand on his leg and closed my eyes because I think I'm going to be sick, and there was a miracle. Another miracle. Ziggy licked at my hand and in one minute . . . one . . . minute . . . he rolled onto his feet. I thought he will make it worse, the break, so I try to look at his leg under my

60

hand and he licks at me again. I took my hand off and I thought, You stupid old woman, you have put your hand on the wrong leg. This one is fine. No blood, no bones poking out. Nothing. But I turn him around and his tail is wagging because he thinks I am playing with him. The other foot was fine too. Not . . . a . . . mark. And Ziggy walked home. Miracle. Praise Got.'

I thought she was crazy. Part of me thought she must have skipped her medication or something but another part of me wanted to believe. And God? God was something that lonely people believed in so they could sleep better at night. I'd never been inside a church. Not once. Never been in a hospital and never been in a church. The few times church people have come to our place trying to sell us stuff, Dad has gone right off at them. He swears at them and tells them to bother someone else. Graham and Tina have a sign on their front gate that says 'No Jehovahs'. Dad has never made a sign. I think he likes going off at them.

'Hard to believe, huh, *schat*? I know, I know. That is my experiment. You have your own experiment and I have mine.'

'Experience,' I said.

'*Ja*, experiment. We are different but we are the same. Sometime you will know something or see something and you won't be able to explain it. There are many, many things from my life that I can not explain.'

I wriggled forward on my chair, then stood up. I thought that if I didn't get going on the apple tree soon I'd miss my ride with Tina. The leather beneath my legs had turned dark with the water from my clothes. I wondered if it would stain.

'Nay. It is fine. Here, sit on the towel. The rain is too heavy for you to work today. Today we talk. Sit. You want coffee?'

I arranged the towel and sat down. She knew my thoughts long before they'd come out of my mouth. She moved into the kitchen. 'I'll pay you to keep an old lady company,' she said, and chuckled.

She made me a coffee — white with two sugars — and sat it on the coaster in front of me. Two windmill-shaped biscuits on a small plate. I had never had coffee before. Mum and Dad drink tea. To Eddy I wasn't a kid. To Eddy I was just another friend. I sat back on the towel and sighed to myself. She was paying me for this?

'So, Dan-ee-el, how old are you? You live in Bellan, *ja*?'

I told her my life story in two minutes. Told her about my grumpy dad and my mum in her vegie garden and my little brother who shares my room. Oh, and Kat. My big sister who lives in another world. Almost forgot her.

'It is good that you have a family. Families break up all the time now. They have forgotten how important it is to bring up kids. The mum or the dad, they go when they get an itch. I feel for the children growing up.'

I thought about my dad and how I wouldn't miss him if he took off. It would be like a huge weight off my shoulders. And Mum's.

'Oh, but you would miss your father if he wasn't there,' she said, as if my thoughts had been words. 'Just because you don't think all the time the same, doesn't mean that you aren't good for each other. Sometimes those people that are hardest to be around teach us the biggest things in life.'

I shrugged and the thought flashed through my mind before I could stop it: how would you know?

She reached for her coffee cup and slurped noisily from the edge. A hint of a smile hung on her lips. She patted her cobweb hair.

'We lived on the Bellan road. Near to where that poor man died under the tractor. Do you remember that? Last year?'

'Mr Lane? That was three years ago at least.'

She snickered. '*Ja*, it probably was.'

'Who bought your house? Was it Graham and Tina?'

'No. Our house was burnt to the ground twenty years ago. There is nothing left. It's all pine trees now.'

I looked at the mental pictures I had of that pine forest — I'd walked through there a hundred times — and I thought I remembered a concrete slab. Yes, a slab and a few broken bricks. I knew where she had lived.

'Skippy saved us. I used to look after animals. All the baby animals off the mothers who were dead by a car. One little baby joey we called Skippy — we called all the baby kangaroos Skippy, after the TV program. You remember? Nay, it was before you were born. Skippy was to be put down the next day because his back legs wouldn't work. When his mum was killed his back was hurt but Kasper and I fed him and looked after him. He slept in an old jumper in the lounge room, hanging on the arm of the chair. He couldn't hop and we decided before we went to bed that night that we would take him to the vet in the morning to be put down.

'Kasper and I were asleep in the house and during the night I heard *hop, hop, hop* down the wooden hallway. I'm thinking to myself, "*Ja*, I'm dreaming, *hoor*." And it came again, the sound *hop, hop, hop*, so I am getting up to find Skippy bouncing in the hallway. It is a miracle and on the ceiling is all smoke. The stove flue had caught alight in the roof while we were sleeping. I wake Kasper and there is a crash from the kitchen and I can see the flames from the bedroom, so I am grabbing Skippy and we're climbing out of the bedroom window and watching the house burn like a big bonfire. True, *hoor*.'

I believed her. I had no reason to, but I believed her. No reason except the tears in her eyes and how her breath caught in her throat. She believed.

'These are my experiments. One day you will have an experiment the same and you will know. You will know that there is more to life than skin and bones and trees. That is how we understand spirit, from experiments. Church teaches people about spirit but they can't really know until they have an experiment of their own.'

I had to go. The gold clock on the cabinet was screaming at me. If I didn't leave right at that moment, I'd be walking the forty kilometres home.

'*Ja*, take a biscuit. Come back again when it is not so raining and work some more,' she said, and stood up. She pulled an envelope from her pocket and handed it to me.

'Don't be silly,' I said. 'I didn't do anything.'

'*Jaaa*. You turned up. Take it. Do you think if you work

64

for McDonald's and nobody comes through the door that they will not pay you? Come again, huh, *schat*? Come and work some more in my garden.'

I took the money and felt guilty about it until I reached the shining street. The sun had poked its watery head between a few heavy clouds and lit up the neighbourhood with a triumphant shine. It had stopped raining and the air smelled wet and alive. The white car with the 'For sale' sign in the window was still sitting on the nature strip. I read the phone number. I ripped the envelope from Eddy open, counted fifty dollars and thought that I might buy that car. Eight hundred and fifty dollars. Would blow a steaming great hole in my savings, but would the water bead like crystals on the bonnet of a car that hadn't been looked after?

It started raining again. Hard. I said the phone number over and over as I jogged to Tina's work. By the time I made it to the ute I was soaked again, but I was singing the phone number over the din of the rain like a madman. Tina was rattling her keys and hurrying from the office with her head bent and eyes squinting. She stopped short of the car when she saw me.

'G'day, Dan. You been for a swim?' she shouted, and laughed.

We dived into the ute.

'Pooh. You smell like a dog,' she said.

I thanked her.

She grunted and looked at me as though I was wearing a possum on my head.

'What?' I asked.

'I do believe I heard you make a joke, Daniel.'

'What's wrong with that?'

'Nothing,' she said.

'Then shut up and drive.'

She roared with laughter and saluted me. 'You in love, Dan? You've got a smile on your face. Your eyes are sparkling.'

'Not likely,' I grumbled. 'I like the rain.'

Tina looked at me sideways.

I struggled not to smile and looked out the window. I forgot the phone number.

# nine

# POSSUM

Michael Fisher had glandular fever. That's what Amy what's-her-name said on the bus. She was talking to Chantelle but everyone could hear. 'The kissing disease', she called it. She said that she might have it. I hoped she did.

She didn't turn up for the bus the next day or for the rest of the week, and by Friday the scabs had started falling off my cheek. It looked like I'd taken an electric sander to my face.

The bus trip seemed quiet without Amy and Michael. Chantelle had the back seat to herself. We were heading home on Friday afternoon, hurtling past Carmine Cemetery, and she caught me staring back at her. I turned, but I thought I saw her pat the seat beside her. She must've been desperate. My gut tingled. She was looking out the window. It gets on Wayne's nerves when kids walk around while the bus is moving.

Chantelle patted the seat. Was she looking at me? I glanced around but there were only a couple of year sevens and Kat on my side of the bus. Kat was elbow-deep in a copy of *Dolly* with the radio blaring in her headphones. Chantelle *must* have been looking at me. I pointed to my chest and whispered, 'Me?'

She nodded and waved me over. I glanced at Wayne and skidded through to sit beside her. Well, on the same seat as her. Could have squeezed another three bodies between us.

'Hey, Dan, what happened to your face?'

'I . . .' I couldn't decide which story to tell her. I cut myself shaving? I got assaulted in the bush? Maybe a new one. A car accident! 'I fell down went boom,' I said.

She chuckled. Her earrings jingled; little horseshoes on chains. 'How? Did you stack your bike? You got a motorbike?'

'No, I haven't got a bike. Wouldn't mind one though. I was running.'

'Yeah . . . And?'

'And someone jumped on my back.'

'Jumped on your back?'

'Yeah.'

'While you were running?'

'Yeah, oh, from a motorbike. They jumped on my back from a motorbike.'

'Fair dinkum? That's a bit vicious. Who?'

68

I shrugged. 'I dunno. I was mucking around and they took it all a bit seriously.'

'They?'

'Yeah,' I said, and my throat squelched as I swallowed. 'Michael and James Sheffield and a few of their mates.'

Her mouth dropped open and she looked at me, wide-eyed, as I told her the rest of the story.

'Too much testosterone. That's what Mum reckons,' she said quietly. 'Did you tell your mum and dad?'

I shook my head.

'Why not? They could have had a word with Mr Fisher.'

I shrugged. The conversation fell into a hole. I wanted to explain why I didn't tell Mum and Dad but the words wouldn't come together. I gripped the seat between my legs. I almost stood up.

Chantelle squinted at me. 'You've changed,' she said. 'It's like a light went out when you were in year six. When Chris . . .'

'Yeah,' I said, before she could finish. 'You're probably right.'

I stood and headed for my seat. Wayne was frowning at me in the rear-vision mirror, pointing for me to sit down. I waved an apology and thumped onto the vinyl. I stared out the window. The sun had started to bake the tall grass flowers on the roadside. The farmers on the flats were bailing the last of the silage. The rain earlier in the week had given them a sense of hope on the radio, but the sun had come out again and they'd gone back to talking about a long hot summer and the whole country burning. I remember them saying the same thing the year before. No matter what the weather is like, they've always got something to complain about. It was unusually hot. It was abnormally dry. A few more hot days and they'd be cutting rough hay before the end of November. That was early.

I picked at a rip in the seat until it was time for Kat and me to get off. Chantelle waved from the back window. She said something to the glass that I couldn't hear. I waved and started walking home. Kat shrugged her pack onto her back and walked to the bus shelter. She'd rather wait for Graham than walk.

Antonio tooted and pulled up beside me, the tyres of the white Commodore hacking on the dirt and covering me in dust. He still looked out of place in a suit and tie. Whenever we worked together he wore the grungiest jeans and old paint-splattered T-shirts.

'Hiya, Dan. How are you? Gawd, what happened to your face?' he said, and stuck his hand out the window.

I laughed and shook his hand. 'Fell down went boom.'

He tossed his head in a silent laugh. 'You want some work? Got a bit of stuff to do at my place when you've got time.'

'Oh, yeah. Suppose.'

'Have you got a minute? I could show you if you like.'

He moved papers and a mobile phone off the passenger seat and I jogged around to get in. I shouted to Kat that I was going to Antonio's place and she waved with the back of her hand.

We cruised into his driveway and parked in front of the house. The gardens looked okay. Nothing much poking through the mulch. Beside the pond was a branch of cypress that had broken off a huge tree and smashed one of his garden statues. It was probably five cars long and as thick as my waist at the splintered end.

'Yep, cut all that up and drag it down to the pile of dead blackberries and burn the lot for me. There's gloves and fuel for the chainsaw in the shed. Jen and I won't be home on Saturday but you don't need us to be here, do you?'

'That'll be fine. Looks easy enough.'

'Can you do it this weekend?'

'Oh, yeah.'

'Good lad,' he said, and slapped me on the arm.

Graham's old red Mazda pulled up at the end of the drive and tooted. I waved to Antonio and ran to the car.

Graham is a wild driver. Fast and all over the road. He doesn't wear a seatbelt. Kat and I always do. The driving is made worse by the fact that Kat and Graham get on better than Kat and anyone else I know — except maybe Mum. Graham taught Kat how to speak sign language when we shifted up to Bellan and they have long danger-ous conversations when we're heading home. I can finger-spell and mime a little but couldn't get my head around signing. Graham and I write notes to each other. Graham and Kat are a blur of hands and over-the-top facial expres-sions. Graham steers with his knee a lot and there have been times on the winding Bellan road when I've wanted to bail out. Thank God his car is an auto. He's never crashed into anything while we've been in the car, but the duco is spotted with panel beater's undercoat — proof enough that it's only luck it hasn't happened.

I remembered the phone number. I thought about the Mitsubishi Scorpion and remembered the number. I asked Kat to see if I could use the phone at Graham's place before we went home and he wanted to know what for, then got all excited when I mimed that I wanted to buy a car.

'What do you want a bloody car for? You can't drive. I'm going to have my licence before you do,' Kat growled.

I shrugged. It was a bargain. I wasn't going to be like Mum and never drive. I wasn't going to be like Kat and wait until I'm twenty before I think about getting my learner's permit.

'Graham said he'd come and check it out for you if you want,' she said flatly.

I patted him on the shoulder and he shrugged and smiled.


A husky-voiced lady answered the phone. She had the shadow of an accent in her words. The car had been her husband's. He'd had a heart attack and died in hospital almost a year before. She said that it was in perfect condition and that I'd be welcome to take it for a test drive. I told her that I didn't have my licence, and for a moment it all seemed like a silly idea. It would be more than a year before I could legally drive it on the road.

'Graham said he wants to come with you and check it out,' Kat shouted from the kitchen.

The lady on the phone said to come over on Sunday. She said she'd be at church in the morning but home in the afternoon. Kat shouted that Sunday would be fine.

I thanked the lady and hung up. I thanked Graham and he shrugged. I thought that there would still be time for me to pull out. I wrote him a note that said someone else might be able to take me on Sunday. He barked like an Alsatian and jabbed a finger at his chest. I shrugged and signed 'Okay'.

Dad was home on Saturday morning and as grumpy as hell. I told Mum about the car and asked her not to tell Dad. I forgot to tell Kat though, and later Dad thumped on the door of the cubby. Tobe and I had been hiding inside while he had his breakfast. The thump made Toby squeal. I stuffed my magazine away and unbolted the door.

'Kat tells me you're thinking about buying a car.'

I shrugged and nodded.

'That's a bit bloody stupid; you can't drive for another year. What are you going to do with it, watch it rust?'

'I was going to work on it and that. Get it really nice. Kat can get her Ls now. You could teach her in it.'

He grunted. 'Won't be really nice for long with your bloody sister driving it.'

I opened my mouth to stick up for Kat and thought that it would have been useless. Dad had made up his mind that it was a stupid idea and I knew I couldn't change that.

'Your bloody money. Better than pissing it against the wall,' he said, and his keys rattled as he walked to the door of his shed.

'Dad?' I yelled.

'What?'

'Would you be able to drop me at Antonio's place? I've got some work to do there.'

'Not now. Maybe this afternoon,' he said.

I listened as he unlocked the door and clomped inside. He bolted the door closed behind him. The curtain screeched as he closed it. I heard the other lock *rasp-clink* open and the drawer slide. The rustling of paper. I knew what was in there. I knew he had a collection of girlie magazines. I'd never seen them, but I knew. I knew that he'd rather read his stick books than be with us.

Toby looked up at me from his table and I felt sick in the guts. The poor little bloke had tears in his big eyes. I knelt down and hugged him. He wiped his face on my shoulder.

'What is it, Tobe?'

'Nothing,' he mumbled into my neck.

My little brother is so beautiful. So perfect. I couldn't understand why Dad would want to be anywhere but with him.

Mum made hot dogs for lunch. I ate seven. Dad asked Toby if he wanted to come for a drive into town and Tobe's eyes nearly popped out of his head.

'Can I come?' Kat asked, and Dad smiled.

'Maybe next time,' he said.

Kat huffed and went to her room.

Toby ran ahead and Dad told him to watch where he was going. 'You coming?' he said to the wall.

'Me?' I asked.

He nodded. 'Didn't you say you wanted a lift?'

I jumped from my chair and slipped into my boots on

74

the way to the car. Mum waved from the kitchen. Kat pulled her curtains closed.

Dad dropped me at Antonio's driveway and said he'd be back in a couple of hours. Toby grabbed me by the shirt and kissed my ear. 'Have fun, Dan.'

The key for the shed was under the pot plant beside the front door. The chainsaw barked into life second pull. I had half a smile on my face as my boot disappeared under white cypress sawdust. Chainsaws are sensible tools. Good tools. The right tool for the job. I'd cut the big bits up and sawn off all the branches in twenty minutes. Cypress cuts like cheese with a nice sharp saw. Sharpened it myself and it didn't look like it had been used since.

The hot afternoon turned sweaty as I dragged the sweet-smelling branches past the old poplars, straight as goalposts, to where I'd stacked the blackberries before winter. The stack had rotted a bit and all the leaves had fallen off, leaving a giant bird's-nest of thorny stems. The cypress squashed the mess some more but by the time I was ready to light it, the pile was twice as tall as me. I looked at the bits of the broken statue. It was busted beyond being glued.

Antonio is a pyro. He keeps kerosene for lighting little fires. He and Jennie rake up all the leaves from the poplars and oaks in autumn. He doesn't believe in composting and feeding his garden with rotting leaves. He burns every-thing, and rather than set one big pile alight, he'll set seventeen wheelbarrow-sized clumps ablaze so the creek and the little valley choke with thick smoke. I couldn't find the kero so I used a bit of the two-stroke for the chainsaw.

About a litre, splashed over the top of the pile so I could see it dripping onto the blackberries. I had played with petrol and matches at home. I knew what would happen. I stood a good distance away and lit matches and threw them at the rainbow-coloured wet on the edge of the pile. The first six matches must have been out by the time they got to the pile, me edging forward with each unsuccessful throw. Lucky number seven. Lucky number seven ignited the fuel and the explosion made me stumble. I felt my shirt flap with the force of it. I could smell burning hair, and there wasn't much on my head to burn. I thought they would have heard it in Carmine. Maybe even felt it. I looked up at the road and around and cursed myself. How stupid was that? Crazy.

The pile was well alight; chugging white smoke into the hot air, crackling and whistling as the branches gave in to the heat. I stared at the flames and thought that they must have been invented for staring into. Off in the distance I could hear the wail of a siren. It was getting louder. Sounded like an ambulance. Maybe a cow cocky had hurt himself. Happened all the time. Then the siren stopped and I could hear a big diesel engine revving hard. It swung into the Bellan road and skidded on the gravel. It was one of the Henning CFA tankers. Hulking red and flashing lights. Must have been a bushfire up our road. It came into Antonio's driveway. Came down the drive and pulled across the neat lawn. Parked right next to me. I heard scuffling in the tall poplar behind me and turned to see a big brush-tailed possum clinging to the trunk, its eyes watering from the smoke. I'd smoked it out of the tree. It didn't look happy.

Men in bright orange overalls filed out of the truck, from the cabin and off the back.

Michael Fisher. He didn't look very sick.

'It's Fairy! Well, who would have guessed, hey?' he said.

My fingers tingled.

A couple of men began unfurling a hose from the side of the truck. Inside the cabin a radio barked some static, then chimed. One of the men climbed back in and garbled something that I couldn't hear into the microphone. A bloke in a yellow hard hat came up to me.

'You lit this then?' he asked.

I nodded. 'Just a bit of burning off.'

'Is Calais here?' he asked.

I shook my head.

'We're going to have to put it out. Bit dangerous on a day like today.'

'Put it out? What for?'

A motor started on the back of the truck.

'It's an illegal fire. We're in a fire restriction period, mate. You didn't get a permit. If this fire got away into that scrub up there . . .' He shook his head and waved with the back of his hand to the foothills in the distance, blue-green with gum trees. 'Half of Henning would go up.'

Michael stood ready with the hose and opened the nozzle on the pile. It hissed and spluttered and the smoke turned to steam.

'You're lucky,' said the bloke in the hard hat. 'Five-thousand-dollar fine for lighting a fire in a fire restriction period. Or one year in jail.'

'Look out, Dad,' Michael shouted.

'What?' the bloke in the hard hat asked. Michael's dad. I could see the same shapes in their faces. Same squinty dark-brown eyes. Same scruffy mud-coloured hair. Same gap between their front teeth. Michael's dad moved back and dragged me with him by the sleeve. I expected to see an ember glowing on the poplar but saw only the possum. I stared in disbelief as Michael screwed the nozzle of the hose until it made a jet and blew the possum off the tree and into the grass.

'Stop!' I shouted. 'Leave it alone.'

I stepped forward and Michael turned the hose on me. My body went rigid as I was instantly soaked. The water splashed in my face and I thought I was going to die. I couldn't breathe. I was drowning. I gasped and frantically clawed at the water stinging my skin.

The pump died. Michael and his dad were chuckling. The breath rasped in my throat.

'Oh, sorry, Fairy. Slipped.'

I panted. I watched them pack up and leave with my arms at my side, drips falling from the tips of my fingers. The siren *whooped* as they pulled onto the Carmine road and I jumped. The sound of the engine faded and I fell to my knees. I thought I was going to scream. The rage stuck in my throat like a chicken bone. I grabbed at the dirt and roared through clenched teeth. Roared and spat at the ground.

I heard the sound of claws on bark and looked up to see the possum climbing up another poplar. The hosing had flattened its fur so it looked as scrawny as a feral cat. I was still watching it when a car pulled into the drive. Antonio and Jennie. I hurried to my feet and collected the chainsaw and fuel can. How would I explain what happened?

'You fall in the creek, Dan? You've been working so hard that you've started to melt,' Antonio said, as he walked down to me. I shrugged. Jennie waved and headed into the house with a bag she'd pulled from the boot.

Antonio surveyed the steaming pile. 'What happened here?'

'The CFA put it out.'

'The what?' he said, and put his hand to his mouth. 'Fire restrictions. They started yesterday.'

'Yesterday?' I clenched my jaw and shivered.

'So they came down to put it out?'

'Yep. Threatened that I should be put in jail or fined five thousand dollars.'

Antonio's dark eyebrows climbed up his forehead. 'Sorry, Daniel. My fault. Slipped my mind,' he said, and kicked at the blackened end of a branch. 'Why didn't they just stand by until it burnt out?'

I shrugged again.

'How did you get so wet anyway?'

I told him the story of Michael and the possum. How Michael had turned the hose on me.

'Are you all right?'

'Yeah.'

He shook his head. 'John Fisher hates my guts. It's political and it goes back to before you were born. He runs the Henning CFA like it's his own private army.'

He picked up a bit of cypress branch and chucked it onto

the pile. 'I think you handled yourself well, Dan. And thanks for doing the work. How much do I owe you?'

He pulled his fat wallet from his back pocket.

'Nah, don't worry about it. I didn't get the job done.'

'Twenty enough?'

'Nah . . . don't . . . ten will be heaps.'

He stuffed a twenty into my palm. 'Some compo for getting squirted in the line of duty. Stay out of Fisher's way.'

'I try to, believe me.'

I sat in the shade of the sycamore at the end of Antonio's driveway and waved away the mosquitoes. Half an hour passed. I could hear hoof-falls crunching on the gravel of the Carmine road before I could see the horse. And the girl. A girl on a tall chestnut with two small dogs running alongside. The horse was walking with its head down. The girl had one hand resting on the saddle; the other lazily swung at flies under the peak of her silly helmet. One of those white horsey helmets with holes in them so the rider's head can breathe. I moved to the roadside for a better look and one of the dogs spotted me and came bounding up, its tail flapping against the side of its body as it arched and licked at my hand.

The dog made me smile. I wished people were that easygoing. I wished everyone would wag their tail whenever they met someone new.

'Hello, Dan,' said the rider.

It was Chantelle. I stood and wiped the dog hair onto my shorts. The little dog jumped and licked at my knuckles.

'Hiya,' I said.

'What are you doing here?' she asked.

'Oh, nothing. Just done a bit of work for Mr Calais. I'm waiting for my dad.'

She pointed to the house. 'You work for the mayor?'

'Yeah. Every now and again. In his garden.'

'Cool. Amazing garden.'

'Yeah.'

The other dog joined in the game of 'jump-up-on-Daniel'.

'Stacey! Rabbit! Get down,' Chantelle growled.

'They're all right,' I said. 'Cute dogs. Which one is Rabbit?'

'The boy.'

I flushed and slapped Rabbit in the ribs like he was a hand drum. His tongue flagged from the side of his mouth.

'What are you doing here, anyway?' I asked.

'Riding, der.'

I shrugged and my face got hot again.

She laughed and I laughed with her.

'That was a bit mean,' she said. 'Like on the bus yesterday. Sorry 'bout that, Dan. I didn't mean to . . . I'm such a bitch sometimes.'

'Nah, that was nothing. You've got some work to do if you want to be a bitch.'

'You reckon?' she said, and laughed.

A pair of gang-gang cockatoos creaked and squawked as they flew overhead. They fly like they're still on their Ls. The male had a head of red feathers and together they swerved and banked like at any moment they were going to crash.

There was a hole in the conversation and I knew she was ready to go. I knew she was ready, and for the first time in my whole life I knew I wanted to go with her.

'All right if I walk with you?' I asked. I held my breath. I suddenly needed to go to the toilet.

'Yeah,' she said. Just like that. 'That'd be cool.'

'Just one sec,' I said, and ran down the drive. Antonio was unloading stuff from the car and I asked him to let my dad know that I'd started walking. Antonio looked up and saw the horse and rider on the road. He smiled and nodded.

I had to walk fast in the afternoon sun to keep up with the horse. Rabbit kept jumping up and licking at my hand. I needed to wee but hung on. I couldn't think of a way to go without making a scene. Sweat ran down the side of my face and tickled my neck.

'Look at you, Dan. Your head is leaking. Do you want to ride for a while?'

'Nah, it's okay. I'll walk.'

She slipped off the horse without stopping. 'Just hold the reins then,' she said. 'Keep walking. I've just got to . . . just got to go to the toilet. I'll catch up.'

Chantelle jogged back the way we'd come and disappeared into the scrub on the roadside. As soon as she was out of sight I dropped my shorts and sighed as the powdery dirt on the side of the road went dark with my wee. The dirt went dark and my head got light with relief. I'd just tucked myself away when Chantelle jogged up behind me and took the reins.

'Come on,' she said. 'Jump up.'

'Nah, I'll walk.'

'Come on, Dan. I'll hold the reins. You get on the back.'

'Both of us? We'll squash your horse.'

'Nah, she doesn't mind, do you, April?' she said, and slapped the horse's neck. 'Left foot in the stirrup, come on.'

I shrugged and lifted my foot into the stirrup.

'Ready? One, two, three.'

I kicked my leg over and nearly threw myself onto the ground on the other side of the horse.

'Sit behind the saddle,' she said, and expertly launched herself into position.

'I haven't got a helmet,' I said. She was so close that I could smell her. Horse sweat and deodorant.

'You can have mine if you want. We'll just walk.'

'Nah, I'll be okay,' I said, but my heart was racing. Thumping hard because I'd never sat on a horse. Drumming in my chest because I hadn't sat this close to a girl since kinder. Chantelle clicked her tongue and April started walking. I grabbed onto the back of the saddle and my finger flicked against Chantelle's jeans. She looked over her shoulder and smiled.

'You won't fall off, Dan. Relax. Hang on to my waist if you want.'

I did hang on to her but I couldn't relax. I breathed little breaths and tried to enjoy the view.

A car scrunched in the gravel behind us and I turned to see the chrome of the P76 shining in the late afternoon sun. No, I thought, not yet, Dad. Just a few more minutes. Just a few more minutes of this closeness might turn my whole world around.

Chantelle walked April to the edge of the road. Dad

cruised alongside. Tobe was hanging out the back window.

'Dan! What are you doing, Dan?' my little brother shouted.

Chantelle's head nearly screwed off to see who was calling.

'My brother,' I said to her. 'What does it look like I'm doing, Tobe?'

'Riding a horsey.'

Dad was smiling. He was looking at the road with his hairy arm on the window and smiling. The fake smile that he uses when we're in company. It's a good disguise. 'Do you want a lift?' he asked.

'Not really,' I grumbled.

Chantelle laughed and pulled April up. Dad stopped the car. Toby scrabbled with his seatbelt. I looked over the side of the horse and searched for a handhold. It was a long way to the ground.

'Hold my hand and slide your other leg over,' Chantelle said.

'No,' I said, and swivelled so that both of my legs were on the left side. 'I'll be right.'

April shook. It started at her hooves and rattled through her legs. The bit in her mouth jangled and I slipped off her side before I was ready. I landed awkwardly and finished up on my bottom in the dirt. Toby squealed with laughter. Dad grunted.

'You okay, Dan?' Chantelle asked.

I stood and dusted myself off. Chantelle was smiling under her silly helmet. My face got hot again and I poked my tongue at her. She laughed.

'Thank you,' I said.

She shrugged. 'See you Monday, I guess.'

I nodded.

She turned April and kicked her into a trot towards Henning. I watched her rise rhythmically in the saddle. It looked like she was dancing. I stared hard at her back. I wanted to remember everything about that ride. Everything about her. She turned and waved. I wanted to be able to see that picture in my mind over and over. I fell asleep with a smile on my face that night.

# ten
# WALLABY

Sunday started out as a hot day. There are some days in Bellan where you can feel the air heating up even before the sun rises. Toby and I played in the cubby until Dad left for work after lunch. Afternoon shift. I walked to Graham and Tina's. Tina's car was under the carport but she was nowhere to be seen. Graham was untangling a big mess of pink baling twine, sweat on his brow. He threw the pile down when he saw me and flicked at it with the back of his hand. He opened the door on his car and flopped in. I climbed into the passenger seat and belted up.

We travelled in silence almost to the end of the road, then Graham started signing to me. He slapped the steering wheel in frustration as he had to finger-spell the message I'd missed again. M-a-r-something, too fast-e-t. I nodded and he groaned and looked out the window. He motioned for me to open the glove box. Pen and paper. He snatched them from my hand. The tyres husked on the gravel of the Bellan road as he steered and wrote. I held on to my seat.

'I have to go to the market to get Tina,' he wrote.

I nodded and gave him the thumbs up. I'd given him instructions on how to get to Concertina Drive and he was going to take us via the Sunday market. That was okay. Hadn't been to the Carmine market for years.

It was hot and packed. Some people smelled shower-fresh, others like sweat and cigarettes. I followed behind Graham, stopping when he bought an old cigarette tin and a cheap set of spanners, and again when he grabbed some bread.

We walked straight past Amy what's-her-name. My tummy tingled. Amy was sitting with her mum at a stall full of plants. I looked away and bumped into a fat man in a blue singlet with a tattoo of a tiger on his shoulder. He shot me a look. I apologised. Amy had sunglasses on. I don't think she saw me. Mustn't have. She would have said something. I followed Graham through all the permanent stalls to the place out the back where people sell things from the boot of their cars. Tina was sitting on a folding chair next to Penny Lane. Penny's daughter, Peta, was sitting at her feet playing a noisy electronic game. Penny was slumped in her seat like someone had deflated her body. Tina smiled and waved. She signed something to Graham, who nodded. Tina rested her hand on Penny's shoulder, then the three of us left for Concertina Drive.

I had butterflies in my stomach. Well, not really butterflies; they were heavy emperor gum moths flapping around in there. I had always been good at saving money and I fondled the huge wad of notes in my pocket. Good at saving, lousy at spending. Never spent more than ten dollars at once since I started working. I craned my head as we flashed past No. 4. Eddy was nowhere to be seen. I tapped Graham on the shoulder and pointed to the car on the nature strip. It looked shinier, cleaner or something. Graham pulled into the driveway and the doors creaked as we got out.

I wanted it. All chrome and flawless white paint that was silky to the touch. The old lady who owned it must have been watching from the window. She came out rattling keys before I'd even thought about going to knock.

She introduced herself and opened the door of the car. Mrs Vos. Hilary Vos. The door didn't creak and it smelled new inside. It looked new. It smelled like freedom. The dead man must have loved his car.

'Who's interested in buying the car?' she asked, and held out the keys. She did have an accent. Graham grunted and took the keys from her. He stepped into the driver's seat.

'I am,' I said. 'I don't have my licence yet so Graham is checking it out for me.'

'You don't drive? Yes, you said that on the phone. But you will drive soon, huh?'

'Next year.'

She looked at me and her eyes pinched. 'You look familiar. Do you live around here?'

'No. I live in Bellan. I work for Mrs . . . I work for Eddy,' I said, and pointed along the street.

Graham started the car and revved the engine hard. Mrs Vos frowned at him. He was looking at the dash and pumping the accelerator. It sounded like a racing car.

Tina gritted her teeth and stuffed her hands into her pockets. She was trying not to shout at him in sign. 'He's hard of hearing,' she said to Mrs Vos.

'Oh,' Mrs Vos said, and stepped closer to the car. 'Is he . . . will he be okay driving the car?'

'Yeah,' I said. 'He's an excellent driver. Just testing the engine.'

Mrs Vos poked her chin at Graham and smiled. 'Let the engine warm up a bit,' she shouted. 'That's what Sidney used to do.'

Tina signed through the windscreen. He shrugged and waved us in. Tina flipped the seat forward and climbed into the back. I pulled my seatbelt on before my bottom had settled into the seat.

Mrs Vos' mouth hung open.

'We'll just go around the block,' I shouted.

She managed a weak smile.

Graham looked at the gear stick and rested his hand on it.

'Hang on,' Tina said. 'I don't think he's driven a manual before.'

There was a harsh rasping metal sound as Graham tried to put it into first gear without the clutch. Tina slapped him on the shoulder and signed for him to use the pedal. His face was red. He nodded. Mrs Vos was peering in his window.

I'm not quite sure how it happened but the tyres made

noise on the grass. One second, the engine was revving and Graham was checking the mirrors, next the tyres were howling and we were almost airborne off the gutter. Then stalled. The engine stopped and the red lights lit up on the dash. I could hear Graham's foot pumping the accelerator. In a flash he realised that the car had stalled and he turned the key without using the clutch. We lurched forward. My head hit the dash. Clutch. Start. Rev, rev, stall. Clutch. Start. Rev, rev, hop, hop, hop along Concertina Drive. I sat low in the seat and braced myself against the footwell. We stalled again at the corner and Graham groaned and slapped the steering wheel. He signed something sharply.

'No darling, it's not a shitbox,' Tina said. 'It takes practice.'

Graham pushed the door open and stepped out. His hair blew around him and he smiled. He threw his hands up in the air and kicked the front tyre. Tina laughed and fumbled with the latch on the driver's seat. She got out and stuffed the smiling Graham into the back seat. I looked at him and he laughed so loud that I wanted to cover my ears. Tina sat in the pilot's position and drove us smoothly around the block. I got my breath back and felt the car underneath me. Smooth ride. No squeaks or rattles. Everything as neat as new. I wanted it.

Tina pulled up smoothly in front of Mrs Vos' place. Eddy was standing with her. Eddy with her cobweb hair and blue and white apron. When she smiled it seemed to start somewhere near the top of her head and probably stretched to the tips of her toes.

'Hello, Dan-ee-el. I thought it was you. You want to buy Mrs Vos' car? Nice car, hey, *schat*.'

I nodded.

'Yeah, tough car,' Tina said under her breath. 'If it can survive Graham, it can survive anything.'

Graham had popped the bonnet and was poking at the engine.

'How much did you say you wanted?' I asked.

'Eight hundred and fifty. I can't go lower than that. It's a good car. Never had an ounce of trouble with it. Sidney's baby it was.'

I grabbed the cash out of my pocket and started counting. Eddy grabbed me by the elbow and pulled me aside.

'Put your money away, *hoor*,' she whispered. 'Never, never pay full price. Never.' She winked at me. 'Hilary,' she began. The rest of the discussion was in Dutch, Hilary standing with her hands on her hips, Eddy resting one hand on the roof of the car.

'All right!' Mrs Vos shouted, and smiled at Eddy. 'You sure know how to pull the strings, Eddy.'

Eddy fluttered her eyelids at me and smiled. 'Six hundred,' she whispered. 'Quick, pay her now before she changes her mind.'

'*Ja*, six hundred. I hope you enjoy the car, young man. Look after it.'

I nodded and promised that I would.

Tina took the keys from the ignition and screwed the car key from the bunch. She handed the rest of the keys to Mrs Vos and I paid her. I unfolded the fifties and it made me tingle. There was no doubt in my mind that Dad would have something to say about it. Something exciting and encouraging. Not! My money. My car. Chantelle would be impressed, I thought. Tina asked if she could use the phone to get a cover note. Something about insurance. Mrs Vos showed her inside. Graham was still poking under the bonnet.

I hugged Eddy and kissed her soft cheek. I couldn't help myself. Eddy chuckled to herself and hugged me back. Just for a second, it felt like I'd hugged her a thousand times. It felt like the most natural thing in the world.

'Thank you,' I said.

'Bah, it was nothing, *schat. Alle beetjes helpen,*' she said, and her eyes shone. 'Every little bit helps. If I'd had a boy, I would have wanted him to be just like you.'

She grabbed my hand, patted it, then kissed it. 'You're the boy what I never had.'

I squeezed her fingers gently and she let my hand go.

'Time for a cup of coffee?' she asked.

'No, I don't think so,' I said, and Graham slammed the bonnet so hard that I jumped. 'My friends are driving me home. I think they want to get going.'

'*Ja*, okay. See you soon, Dan-ee-el,' she said, and started walking home. There was a spring in her step. I wondered how old she was. Who could tell? She may be sixty, could be eighty and it didn't matter at all. She walked like she was happy to be alive. I think she *was* happy to be alive.

Graham wanted the keys so he could drive my new car home and Tina wouldn't give them to him. He grunted and huffed and eventually drove his own car. Mrs Vos gave me some paperwork. Registration transfer. Tina explained that I had to fill it in and mail it to the RTA in Carmine to have the registration changed into my name. Mrs Vos signed it too and Tina waved to her as we drove off.

'Who was that old lady?' she asked as we drove under the steam shadow of Hepworth B. Toby called the power stations 'cloud factories'. The cooling towers couldn't pump clouds out fast enough that hot afternoon; they turned to invisible vapour on the other side of the road.

'Oh, she's the lady I work for. Eddy. She lives down the road from Mrs Vos.'

'She saved you two hundred and fifty dollars. She's a good mate to have. Does she pay you when you work for her?'

'Yeah. She pays me heaps.'

'Oh yeah?' she said, and I could hear her mind ticking over. 'Just be careful she doesn't rip you off.'

My head jolted backwards in surprise. 'Eddy wouldn't rip me off. She's as honest as . . . as honest as sunshine!'

Tina shrugged. She gripped the steering wheel. 'Great car. Got yourself a bargain, Dan. A ripper.'

She flicked on the radio and it sounded so good. Speakers in the front and the back. The radio station fuzzed loudly as we drove under a scribble of high-voltage power-lines, then came good as we moved into the farmland.

Tina pointed with one finger off the steering wheel. At first I thought she was waving to someone, then I spotted what she had seen. A plume of creamy-brown smoke was being held to the ground by the hot wind. There was a fire at Henning. I felt the car speed up. It was in the foothills, probably farmland, and a long way from our homes, but too close to ignore. As we approached we could tell that the fire hadn't crossed the Bellan–Carmine road. I could see the flashing lights and as we got closer, the hulking firetrucks. There were six units that I could see, fighting the fire front in a distant paddock. The front flashed orange and gold through the smoke that blew over the road and my heart sped up at the sight of it. Another three tankers sat on the side of the road. Two had 'Henning' written on the side in crisp white letters; the third was over from Handley Dell.

A bloke in yellow overalls waved us down. 'Where you heading?' he asked as he leaned on the driver's door.

'Bellan,' Tina said, and pointed down the road. Somewhere in all the smoke was the turn-off.

'Oh. Okay. Take it easy through the smoke,' he said, and slapped the roof.

'Everything under control?' Tina asked.

'Yeah. Will be shortly. The wind isn't helping much.'

'How did it start?'

'Dunno,' he said flatly. 'Chief seems to think it was a bit suspect.'

Another car pulled up behind us.

'Take it easy,' the bloke said, and slapped the roof again.

Tina drove into the smoke and it filled the car in an instant with a sweet grass-fire smell. She wound her window up and I did mine. She drove slowly until we reached the dirt of the Bellan road, then gunned it. The smoke was high over that part of the road, staining the sunlight orange. My little car handled the corners like the wheels were magnets and the road was made of steel. I thought about taking it for a drive when I got home, just up and down our driveway. Dad wouldn't be home until late. Mum wouldn't mind. Maybe she'd let me take it on the road. Just the quiet Bellan road.

Tina was pushing my car through the s-bends just before Penny's place when she sucked in a breath and swerved. Thump! Something went under the back wheel and my head hit the roof as the car bounced. She skidded to a stop.

'Shit,' she said.

'What? What was that?'

'A wallaby,' she said, and leaned on the steering wheel. Her neck was red and the muscles in her jaw twitched. 'Sorry, Dan.'

I jumped out of the car and saw the wallaby through whirling dust clouds. It was on the edge of the road. Its legs kicked at the blood-covered grass. Its head was the wrong shape. I realised as I got closer that the sandy lump on its flattened jaw was an eye. Must have run straight over its head. I stood there with my hands hanging by my sides and wanted to be sick. Wanted to throw up the horrible feeling that I was responsible for killing the wallaby. God, I hoped it died soon. Its side heaved and blood exploded from its smashed nostrils. I took a step back. Tina sat in the car with the engine idling, her head still resting on the steering wheel. The exhaust was hot and sharp in my nose. I may not have been driving but it was my car that had done the damage. The wallaby stopped kicking but its skin twitched and rippled. It was a boy. I could see his scrotum hanging against his leg. Good, I thought. No pouch. I wouldn't have to check for babies. I wouldn't have to find a hairless joey and deal with it. Look after it or put it out of its misery. It was a boy. Good.

I stared at the mangled head. My eyes glazed and I lost the sense of time passing. Tina eventually wound her window down.

'Is it okay?' she asked.

'It's dead,' I said.

She wound the window up.

I tentatively grabbed the wallaby by its bristly tail and dragged it to the edge of the embankment. It didn't kick or twitch; its limbs were loose with fresh death. I rolled it under the dogwoods and down towards the creek. It tumbled and slapped out of sight. The blood on the grass was already beginning to dry and darken. Blowflies buzzed around my head. I went back to the car.

'Is the car okay?' Tina asked.

'I didn't look.'

Tina looked at me, her cheeks wet and her eyes red. 'Sorry, Dan.'

'Nothing you could have done. It happens. Don't worry about it.'

She sniffed and put the car into gear.

'It died quickly,' I said.

I didn't feel like racing up and down the driveway anymore. Tina parked the car beside the cubby. I checked it over and she just stood there. I thanked her. She didn't say anything. She walked home.

Toby had been playing with a bucket of water and his bare body glistened. He had grass stuck to his leg and in his hair.

'Whoah! Dan, whose car is it? Is it yours?'

I nodded.

'Cool! You can drive me to echidna.'

'To where?'

'Echidna,' he said, and looked at me with his head on the side and his eyes pinched. 'You know . . . where I go with Peta and Penny. In Henning.'

'Kinder,' I said, and chuckled.

He squealed. 'Yeah, kinder. What did I say? Echidna. What's echidna?'

'You know, the spiky little animals. We saw one on the road. They eat ants.'

He squealed again and slapped his forehead.

'Could you drive me to kinder now, Dan?'

'No,' I said. 'It's nearly teatime. There's no kinder today, it's Sunday.'

'The next day?'

'No, mate. I'm not allowed to drive it on the road yet. I'm not old enough.'

He looked at me, puzzled. 'When will you be old enough?'

'Next year.'

He looked at his foot. 'How many sleeps?'

I laughed. 'Heaps. You'll be at school then.'

'Cool, you can drive me to school! Huh! That rhymes . . . cool and school, cool and school.'

I brushed the grass off his wet body and sat him in the

passenger seat. Mum came out, wiping her hands on a tea towel.

'That's pretty flash, Dan,' she said, her eyes wide. 'How much did you pay for it?'

'Six hundred.'

'You spent six hundred dollars?'

I nodded. 'She wanted eight fifty. It's a good car.'

'I can see that. I thought it would be worth a couple of thousand. You did all right for yourself.'

Kat came out and ran her hands over the duco. She purred and sat in the driver's seat. 'Nice wheels, Dan,' she said. 'Did you buy it from the old lady you were working for?'

'Nah. Another old lady down the road. Mrs Vos.'

'How much?'

I told her and she whispered 'Six hundred dollars' to the dash.

She tapped the steering wheel. 'Don't suppose I'll be allowed to drive it.'

'Not you, Katty. You'll probably smash it into a tree or run over a chicken,' Tobe said, and we laughed.

'That's not very nice, Toby Fairbrother,' Kat said as she slapped him on his bare knee. Tobe grabbed her arm and licked it. She groaned and he grumbled a laugh to himself. Kat looked at me, her eyes cool. It was the first time I'd looked into her eyes for years. Maybe even since we shifted. Forever. It wasn't her obnoxious little brother she was looking at. She looked at me like she was actually waiting for me to answer her. Like what I was about to say actually mattered. She was wearing a summer dress with no shoes. Her hair hung loose over her shoulder and it struck me how pretty she was.

'What?' she asked, and looked away.

'What what?' I asked.

'Why are you looking at me all weird?'

'I'm not looking at you . . .'

'You were,' she said, and smiled.

I shrugged.

'Well, can I?' she asked.

'Yeah, of course you can. You've got to learn in something.'

She sat back in the seat with her mouth open. 'Serious?'

I shrugged again. 'You'll be waiting forever if you want Dad to teach you in the other car.' She nodded.

'Cool,' Toby shouted. 'Can I drive it, too?'

'Yeah,' I said. 'When you get a bit bigger.'

'Cool! Like when I finish kinder and go to school?'

'Few years yet, mate.'

He looked at Mum. 'How many sleeps is that?'

Mum laughed. She dusted the roof with her tea towel. 'Would I be able to drive it?' she asked.

I thought she was joking but in her eyes she looked frightened.

'Yeah. Course you can.'

Kat looked at her through Toby's window. 'You serious, Mum?'

'Yeah. I've always wanted to drive,' she said, and I got a flash of Dad screaming at her the last time she'd driven. It was a crackly old image but I remembered.

Kat must have had the same picture in her head. She

grumbled, mostly to herself, but we could hear her well enough. 'I wish someone would come and take Dad away in a box and fix him up. Give him a new head. One that hasn't got a broken "happy".'

'That's not very nice, Katty,' Tobe said, and slapped at the dress that covered her knee. She licked him and he squealed.

Mum's eyebrows jumped. 'No,' she said. 'That's not nice. Be careful what you wish for.'

# eleven
# PIG

It was just getting light when a car crunched up the driveway next morning. Kat was in the shower. Dad was in bed. Mum was making lunches in the kitchen and I heard her gasp. I saw her put her hand over her mouth. She ran along the hall to the front door. The door we never use. I dropped my spoon into my bowl and followed her. Looked over her shoulder.

Two policemen got out of the divisional van and pushed their hats on. I thought they'd come to the wrong house. How ironic was that? The police coming to *us* for directions! They came to the dusty porch and spoke quietly to Mum.

'Sorry to disturb you. Is Steven Fairbrother in?' the tallest one asked.

'Wha—? Yes. He's asleep. He's just come off afternoon shift.'

There was a commotion in Mum and Dad's bedroom. I heard the window scrape open and the flywire screen rattle.

The shorter policeman looked down the hall, then looked at the tall one. The tall one nodded and the short one ran around the side of the house. 'He's here! Give us a hand, Jerry?'

The tall cop ran to his mate and I heard Dad groan. I couldn't move. I don't think I wanted to move. Mum had a knuckle in her mouth. The blood had drained from her face and she was shaking. The cops brought Dad to the front door. He was in his white undies. I couldn't remember the last time I'd seen his hairy body. The short cop had Dad's arm bent behind his back. Dad's face was squashed like he was about to cry.

'What's this about?' Dad bawled.

'Are you Steven Fairbrother?'

'Yeah. What's this about?' he asked. The corners of his mouth were white with spittle.

'We have a warrant for your arrest, Mr Fairbrother.'

'Why? What have I done? I haven't done nothing.'

'Then why climb out the window?' the little cop asked gently.

Dad shook his head. 'I dunno . . . I . . .'

'Don't try and explain here, mate. Save it for later,' Jerry, the tall cop, said. 'Now, do you want to travel in your Y-fronts or shall we ask Mrs Fairbrother to get you some clothes?'

Mum shivered and took her knuckle out of her mouth. 'I'll get some clothes,' she said. She brushed by me and I rocked out of my daze. It was like a dream until then. Dad was in trouble. Big trouble. I didn't want to cry. There was nothing to say. He was probably going to jail for whatever he'd done. I almost walked back in to finish my breakfast. Mum came out with a pair of Dad's black tracksuit pants and a green T-shirt. She handed them to Jerry, who handed them to Dad.

'I'm going to let your arm go, Mr Fairbrother, so you can get dressed, okay? Please don't do anything silly.'

Dad nodded. The little cop let him go and he stretched his arm out and screwed his face up. He got dressed in a hurry and asked Mum for some shoes. 'My work boots. They're at the back door.'

Mum got his boots and a pair of thick socks and handed them to Jerry, who handed them to Dad.

Dad was dressed. He stood with his arms at his sides and looked at Mum. She looked old. Older than Eddy.

'Sorry, love,' Dad said.

Mum nodded sharply. Bit late for that, I thought.

The little cop took Dad by the elbow and led him to the back of the van. Dad stepped inside. He didn't fight. He didn't kick or scrabble or shout. He knew why they were taking him away.

Mum and I watched the van disappear along the Bellan road, then I took Mum by the elbow and led her into the dining room. I sat her down on a chair.

'What was all that about?' I asked.

Kat came into the kitchen in her school dress with a towel wrapped around her head.

'I don't know, Dan. I honestly have no idea,' Mum said. Her voice was thin like her throat was cramped.

'What?' Kat asked as she poured some cornflakes into a bowl.

'The police just came and got Dad.'

Kat poured the milk. 'Yeah, yeah.'

'It's true!' I said.

Kat put a spoon into her bowl and walked to Mum and Dad's bedroom. She came back pulling her wet hair into a ponytail with half a smile on her face. 'Really?'

Mum nodded.

'Cool!' Kat said, and slumped into her chair to eat.

Mum stood up slowly. 'Get out, Katrina. Get out of my sight. Now!'

'Mum . . . I haven't finished my —'

'Out. Now.'

'My lunch . . .'

'Go!' Mum screamed.

Kat grabbed her school bag and hurried out the door.

Mum was breathing fast.

'It's not Kat's fault, Mum, Dad treats her like . . .'

'You go too, Dan. Get going. Go and look after your sister,' she said.

'She'll be all right.'

'Go!' she shouted.

'What about Tobe?'

'He'll be fine. Just go. I'll see you tonight.'

I grabbed my bag and ran. Ran out the door and caught up with Kat. There were tears in her eyes and she was laughing. She grabbed my hand and squeezed it. She wiped her eyes on the sleeve of her dress.

'Isn't that just the best bit of news you've ever heard?

The worst best bit of news ever. God, look at me, I'm laughing and crying at the same time.'

I nodded. I wasn't crying. Dad and I hadn't seen eye to eye for years and the thought of him being out of my life for a while made me feel like rubbing my hands together. I wasn't laughing either. How would we pay the bills and what would we say to Toby? I felt numb.

We didn't say a thing to Tina in the ute. She asked me about the car and I thanked her again for driving it home for me.

Kat squeezed my knee. 'Great car.'

We drove through the corner with the bloodied grass.

'Any damage?' Tina asked.

'No. Not a mark.'

Kat looked through the back window. 'What happened?'

'Hit a wallaby on the corner back there.'

'In this?' she asked, and patted the dash of the ute.

'No, in my car.'

'Your car? Was the wallaby okay?'

'Killed it.'

'Killed it?'

'Yup.'

'Gross.'

Michael and Amy weren't on the bus again. My face had almost healed. I'd been waking up with flakes of scab on my pillow. The skin underneath was pink and a bit shiny but I had to stand close to the mirror to notice it.

Chantelle sat on her own at the back of the bus. I looked

over my shoulder at her and she patted the seat again. Kat winked at me as I stepped past her. My tummy fluttered.

'How's your bum?' Chantelle asked.

'My what?'

'When you slid off April's back. Did you hurt yourself?'

'Nah,' I said, and she laughed.

'What did you get up to on Sunday?'

'Nothing much. Went to the market. Bought myself a car. Normal stuff.'

'You what?' she squealed.

I told her the story about getting my Mitsubishi Scorpion. I wanted to tell her about Dad and how happy-sad I felt about him being taken away, but Kat flashed me a look over her shoulder. I wouldn't have been able to find the words anyway.

'Did you see the fire yesterday?' Chantelle asked.

'Yeah . . .'

'It was on my uncle's place. Do you know the Mitchells?'

I shook my head.

'Someone lit it deliberately.'

'Yeah? We drove through the smoke coming back from Carmine and one of the CFA blokes said that it was a bit suspect.'

'They found some sort of little fire bomb.'

We were quiet for a minute and looked across the farmland. Wouldn't take much to set the whole area alight if someone really wanted to.

'That's a bit scary,' I said.

Chantelle nodded.

Kat got called up to the office on the PA twice that day. Once right at the start of lunch, then again halfway through fifth period. I was in maths. I'd finished all the set work and all of the homework and I was bored out of my brain. I scratched a star on the underside of my left arm with the point of my compass. Didn't make it bleed, just made the skin white and a few minutes later it came up in a neat star-shaped welt. At first I thought I'd just write Chantelle's initials, but the scratching felt sort of nice and I had the better part of the period to fill so I wrote 'Chantelle' on the pale underside of my forearm. I'm not even sure why I did it. It wasn't like we were going out or anything. She was probably lonely; with Michael and Amy away she didn't have anyone else to gasbag with. Not that I minded. We weren't going out but Chantelle was the closest thing to romance that I'd ever had in my life. I checked a few times to see if anyone was looking but nobody watches the nobody. Dweebs don't attract much attention. That's probably the only advantage of being a dweeb.

I thought about going to Eddy's that afternoon to pull out the apple tree but I was desperate to get home. I wanted to look at Mum's face, and Toby's, and know that they were okay. That we were okay. That our family would survive without Dad. Eddy would have been the only person in the world who could make any sense out of Dad being taken away. I wished I had her phone number. I didn't even know her last name.

Kat looked different. There was something different about her eyes. She looked wild and satisfied in the same breath, like she'd found out what she was getting for Christmas and it was something she'd always wanted. Her hair was different. It wasn't pulled back. It blew into her face as she stepped onto the bus to go home. She shook it casually over her shoulder and showed Wayne her bus pass. She sat in her usual seat and waved to somebody through the window. Jake. Jake Teychenne. He waved back, then scanned the crowd. He blew her a kiss. Jake Teychenne blew my sister a kiss. Jake with the eyebrow ring and the gaudy silk boxers poking out of the top of his grey school pants. The school shirt with the tails cut off so it couldn't be tucked in, even if Mr Grimshaw, the principal, had tried to do it himself. Jake with the dark goatee that made him look more like a teacher than a student.

I was still looking at Kat with my mouth hanging open when Chantelle darted past to sit on the back seat. I watched her pull her dress over her knees. I wanted to see her pat the seat but she just smiled at me. There was a thump on the window beside her. She stood up and opened the vent and tried to stick her head out. It wouldn't fit. I could see Amy what's-her-name jumping up and asking for something. She wasn't in uniform and she didn't look very sick — bad news. Chantelle looked at Wayne, then handed her bus pass to Amy through the window — bad news. The next thing, Amy was on the bus and thumping along the aisle to sit next to Chantelle — very bad news.

I waited until the bus got moving, then I slipped in beside Kat.

'What happened to you today?' I asked.

'Nothing,' she said. She had a dreamy look in her eyes.

'Why did you get called up to the office?'

She looked at me and screwed up her nose. 'None of your business. Nick off.'

I shrugged and went back to my seat. I guessed that the nice Kat had died again during the day. Caught up in something that I'd find out about in time if it was important.

There was a roadblock on the road to Henning. An RTA car was parked over the white line and a bloke who looked like a half-baked policeman was directing all the traffic down the road to Handley Dell. Wayne had a few words to the bloke and turned towards Handley.

'Der. Where are you going?' Amy shouted at the window.

'All the traffic is being diverted. There's a fire,' Wayne said, matter-of-fact.

'Good one,' Amy muttered.

We had to drive around the Handley high-level storage dam and the smoke wafted across the water like a grubby mist. We'd just crossed the dam wall when Wayne pulled to the side of the road and turned the engine off. He tried to start it again and I realised that he hadn't stopped it; it had just died.

'What is it now?' Amy whinged.

Wayne cranked the engine again. *Whir, whir, whir.* Nothing.

'We're going to stop here for a minute while we get another bus,' Wayne said. 'This one's broken.'

A collective moan.

'I need a volunteer,' Wayne said, and a few kids shouted 'Me, me'.

I stuck my hand up. Drive while he pushes? Crank the engine while he's at the back looking at the motor? Keep everyone under control while he goes for help?

'You,' he said, pointing at me. 'Fairy, isn't it?'

'Daniel,' I said under my breath.

He waved me to the front of the bus.

'I'm not allowed to leave the bus,' he began. 'And I need someone to nip down to the next house and call the bus line for me. You reckon you can handle that?'

I shrugged and nodded. 'Easy.'

He scribbled the number on the back of an old ticket. 'Now is the time when I wished I had one of those stupid mobile phones. Probably wouldn't work here anyway.'

I huffed a laugh as he handed me the ticket.

'Hurry, Fairy,' Amy shouted. 'I don't want to be sitting here all afternoon waiting for *you*.'

'Kindly put a lid on it or you'll be walking,' Wayne said.

I could see the roof of the house from the bus; the rest of it was obscured by garden. It was about a kilometre off and I jogged the whole way. There was a blue car under a steel carport but it wasn't until I'd knocked on the door that I recognised it. Eddy's friend. It looked like . . . what's-his-name's car.

The tall man with the scruffy grey hair answered the door. I remembered his name.

'Hello, Luke,' I said, and smiled.

'*Ja*, hello. I know you! You're Eddy's friend. The nature boy. Daniel, isn't it?'

'Yeah!' I said excitedly. It was good to be remembered.

Luke sniffed the wind. 'There is a fire?'

I nodded. 'Just near the intersection on the Carmine road.'

'*Jaaa?*' he said, and looked across the dam. 'Pretty safe here. Has to jump across the dam before it can get to my place.'

I looked across the dam and thought that he had a postcard view from his front door. Smoky postcard.

'Come in, come in. Why are you here? How can I be helping you?'

I stepped inside. The house was tidy and well lit but it smelled like dog. It smelled so much like dog that my nose wrinkled and I had to rub it.

'Our bus has broken down. The school bus. Just near the dam wall. I was wondering if I could use your phone to call for another bus?'

He stood beside me, smiling, with his hands by his sides. 'Sure!' he said. 'Here is the phone in the lounge room.'

A dog let out a muffled bark from another part of the house.

'Shush, Diamond,' Luke growled. 'It is only Daniel.'

He ushered me into a room that was more like a hothouse than a lounge room. There were indoor plants in pots on every shelf and benchtop. Large palms stood beside the couch and several pots hung from the ceiling above the television.

'Do you have the number?' Luke asked.

'Yep,' I said. I found the phone amongst the greenery on a side table and called the bus company. The woman who answered listened intently, asked where we were, then said thank you, twice. She said another bus would be there in fifteen minutes. I thanked her and she thanked me again.

'All right, Daniel?'

'Yep, all arranged,' I said. 'Fifteen minutes.'

'Ah, good. You can come and see my place.'

'I have to get back to the bus.'

'*Ja?* What for? You have done your bit, haven't you?'

'I . . . I have to tell the driver.'

'Come. Look for five minutes then I'll drive you up. They won't be going anywhere.'

I chuckled and shrugged.

Luke led me into the kitchen and through to the back door. He let his dog out, a smelly old hunting dog that sniffed at my ankles and held its tail straight. One step from the back door and we were in the vegetable garden. Neat rows of lettuces and tomatoes with green fruit on them already. It was twice the size of our garden and we always had enough vegetables for the five of us. Now we'd have more than enough for the four of us.

'Beautiful garden. What do you do with all the vegetables?'

'Give them away to my friends, mostly. Always have enough for me and Diamond to eat, and for *Zwarte Piet*.'

He raised one eyebrow and put a finger to his lips. 'Listen,' he whispered. Then he said loudly, '*Ja*, where is my Piet? Piet, where are you?'

I listened. From beyond the vegie garden came a snuffle and grunt. *Grunt, grunt, grunt.* Luke strode along the path through the middle of the garden and stopped at a low fence that housed his pig. It was huge. I could have saddled

112

it up and ridden it. It snuffled against the wire as Luke scratched the back of its head.

'Daniel, this is my friend *Zwarte Piet* — Black Peter. Santa's little helper. I bought him to have for Christmas dinner. That was nearly ten years ago.'

Piet looked up at me and wagged one of his floppy ears. I scratched him on the back of his head as Luke had done and he sniffed at my wrist. We'd never had pigs. Dad said they stunk. Black Peter didn't stink. Well, not as much as Diamond.

'Are you going to eat him?'

'Nay. What do you reckon? Could you make bacon from one of your best friends? Nay, he turns all my scraps into beautiful compost.'

Yeah, pig medicine; turn everything into a resource.

We walked back along the path and I admired Luke's celery, growing with newspaper wrapped around them to keep the stems pale and tender.

'Do you give Eddy any vegies?' I asked.

'*Ja*, she is my best customer,' he said, and laughed to himself.

I looked at him. Eddy grew more than enough vegies for herself.

He sighed. 'She is a beautiful, beautiful woman, that Eddy.' He stared at his work boots. 'You can see the love in her eyes.'

I nodded, though I didn't really get what he meant. I saw wisdom and understanding in her eyes, and generosity and a sort of all-knowing glow. I didn't see love. Maybe I didn't know what love looked like.

I thought about my family and my stomach clenched. 'I have to get going. I can walk back to the bus.'

'Nonsense. I will drive you,' Luke said, and led me by the elbow along a path that took us down the side of his house to the carport.

The kids were everywhere when we arrived. Wayne sat in the shadow of the broken bus and smoked. Luke introduced himself and said that we'd used his phone to organise another bus.

'Good lad,' Wayne said, and kicked at my boot.

'Did you get lost, Fairy? What took you so long?' Amy shouted from a vent window at the back of the bus. Her arm hung outside.

Luke and Wayne looked at her. She pulled her arm in. Luke started chatting to Wayne about the bus and the fire. I wandered to the dam.

Kat was with a few of the year sevens on the rocks at the edge of the dam. She had her dress up, her runners off and her feet dangling in the water. She still had that blissed-out look on her face. It scared me. It wasn't the sort of look I would have expected to see on the face of someone whose father had just been taken away by the police. I guess my face wouldn't have looked much different. They took my dad away and I went to school. I sat on a rock beside Kat and pulled my boots off.

'Why are you so happy?' I asked.

'Your feet stink,' she said.

I thought about dipping my toes in the water but my heart started beating hard and I felt like I was going to fall

114

in. I slipped my boots back on again and hopped to higher ground. Kat smiled.

Chantelle appeared beside me. Amy hopped across the rocks and stopped next to her.

'You going in, Fairy?' Amy asked, and laughed.

'Nah, too cold,' I said, and shaded my eyes from the smoky sunlight with my hand.

'You're not supposed to swim up here,' Chantelle said.

'Me and Michael do all the time,' Amy said. 'We went skinny-dipping last summer.'

Kat looked over her shoulder and grunted at Amy.

'What?' Amy asked. 'Not like you've ever been skinny-dipping, hey, Katrina?'

Chantelle shot Amy a look.

'What?' Amy asked again. 'She wouldn't have. She's got no friggin' life, like Fairy here. Runs in the family, doesn't it, mate?'

I looked at her and wanted to spit. I wanted to shove her into the water. Into the bottomless black-blue of the Handley dam and pelt her with rocks until she went under.

Amy stepped across and grabbed my wrist. 'What does it say here?'

I'd forgotten my scratched tattoo. I tried to snatch my arm away but she'd already seen it. She'd read the word. She'd caught a glimpse of a part of me that was so private, I hardly knew it existed.

'Haa!' she squealed, and looked at Chantelle.

I started walking to the bus.

'Did you see it? Did you see that? He's got your friggin' name scratched into his arm!'

She squealed so loud that a few people who had stayed near the bus looked over.

'Whooo! Fairy's hot for you, mate. You wanna know what the piss-funniest thing is? He spelt your name wrong. He can't even spell your name. Haa!'

She was squealing laughter and hooting. I wanted to stop her. I wanted to hurt her. Break her. I felt sick.

One step then the next across the rocks and into the shadow of the bus. I could hear the rumbling of a diesel engine and the replacement bus appeared across the dam wall.

'*Ja*, here she comes,' Luke said, and rattled his keys. 'What happens now to this bus?'

'Hopefully there's a mechanic on board. Hopefully the problem is something minor. Hopefully he'll be able to get it going,' Wayne said.

Kids were thumping onto the busted bus to get their bags and stuff. Kat hopped over the rocks barefooted. Amy was giggling to herself and shaking her head. She tripped up the step and slammed into the door. Ended up on her knees, groaning in the stairwell. I looked at Chantelle. She had her hand over her mouth and her eyes were smiling. I didn't laugh. Well, not out loud.

This day was going down in the Daniel Fairbrother hall of fame as one of the worst on record. I sighed as I climbed into Graham's car. He'd waited for us in Henning for almost an hour. He's good like that. The first thing he asked Kat was something about the police. She signed something at a million miles per hour and I only caught one word — the letter 'f' signed twice. Father. Graham's mouth dropped open and he shook his head. Kat nodded. Graham touched his lips and moaned like a sick cow. He signed something else and Kat shrugged. It hadn't been a breakfast nightmare. It was real. If Graham had seen the police, then my dad had definitely been taken away.

There was crazy laughter coming from Graham and Tina's kitchen window. Crazy little-brother laughter. Tina's ute was in the drive. We followed Graham up the front stairs and he looked back at us, puzzled. We normally just head home. Graham couldn't hear Toby laughing but somehow he knew what was going on. He nodded and pointed inside.

Mum asked where we'd been and the hand holding her cup of tea shook.

Toby had an emu chick in his arms. Black stripes and grey downy feathers, oversized beak and haunting brown eyes. Its beak hung open and its neck puffed and flattened.

'I think we'd better put it back in its box now, Tobe,' Tina said.

'It's gorgeous,' Kat said. I'd never heard Kat use the word 'gorgeous' about anything. 'Where did it come from?'

'One of the guys at work found it on the side of the road at Milara. Its dad was hit by a car,' she said.

I almost laughed at the irony of it. I wondered if it was a police car that had killed it.

'Poor thing,' Toby said, and snuggled his face into its downy back before putting it into the cardboard box from a TV. 'It smells like fruit. Where's its mum?'

'Don't know, mate,' Tina said. 'The mum clears off after

the eggs are laid. The dad does the sitting on the nest, incubating, and looks after the chicks once they hatch.'

Just like our family, I thought. Not! Mum's lips smiled but her eyes looked older and grey instead of blue. She hugged Kat and apologised in her ear for what she had said that morning. Kat patted her back and said that she'd forgotten about it.

We walked home in the eerie orange light of smoke shadow. A bushfire afternoon. I walked on one side of Mum, Kat on the other and Toby ran ahead singing 'Where is Pointer?' to himself and doing the actions. Mum told us that she had spoken to Dad on Tina's phone.

I held my breath. I think Kat did too.

'He's not coming home. Not yet, anyway. They're still interviewing him.'

Kat sighed. I couldn't tell if she was happy or sad. Probably both, like me.

'What did he do?' Kat asked.

Mum shrugged. 'Who knows? He's certainly not telling me.'

'He knew he'd done something wrong,' I suggested.

'You reckon?' Kat asked.

'He didn't fight. He just let them put him in the back of the van.'

Mum and Kat were quiet. Toby sang.

'It certainly explains a few things,' Mum sighed.

'Yeah,' Kat said, and took Mum's hand.

'What things?' I asked.

'You know, why he's been behaving the way he has. He hasn't always been like that. He wasn't always a total grump.'

Kat grunted. 'Yes, he was.'

'No,' I said. 'I remember when he took me fishing when we were in Watson. I remember it like it was last week. He laughed. He told me fishing stories.'

'Yeah? I don't remember anything like that,' Kat said, and flicked the hair over her shoulder. 'Are we going to be okay?'

Mum grabbed my hand as well and shrugged. Her face cramped. 'I don't know,' she said. She stopped walking and sobbed. Kat hugged her. I squeezed her hand.

'We'll be okay, Mum. We'll find the money that we need and I can do the stuff that Dad did, like getting firewood and that,' I said. 'We'll be okay.'

'He might be back tomorrow. Who knows?' Mum said.

It was like Kat hadn't heard her. 'Things are going to change, though. We'll play our music loud and, when we can afford it, we'll get a TV.'

'Yeah,' I said. 'And get the phone connected.'

'I want a Playstation Two,' Toby yelled.

Mum laughed and wiped her nose. 'What's a Playstation Two, Tobe?'

He came running back. 'I don't know but Damon's got one. Damon at kinder. They're the best.'

I took Toby's hand and jogged up the driveway. The birds in Dad's aviaries were chattering and flapping against the wire. I told Toby to wait on the drive. Next to the car. The P76. Dad's car. I ran into the house and called, 'Dad?' Loud enough so anyone in the house could hear but not so loud that Toby would. The house creaked in reply. I chucked my bag on the lounge-room floor and ran into

Mum and Dad's bedroom. The sheets were pulled back and the bed was empty. Dad's keys sat on the bedside table. Reflected orange sunlight from somewhere made them glint and I took them in my hand. I felt their weight, jingled them, then covered them with my hand. Stuffed them deep into the pocket of my school shorts. They sounded like Dad. I bolted past Mum and Kat in the hallway. Tobe was still waiting by the P76.

'What are you doing, Dan?' Mum asked.

'Nothing,' I yelled, and waved over my shoulder at her.

I asked Toby to come with me and we sat at the door of the first of the four aviaries.

'Dad's gone away, mate,' I said.

'Yeah. I know. Mum said. She said he mightn't be back for ages and years and years.'

'Are you okay?'

He poked his bottom lip out and shrugged. 'Yeah. Fine.'

I looked at his smooth skin and smiled. It was official. I'd looked after Toby since he was a baby. I'd changed his nappy for Mum and fed him and got him in the bath. When he hurt himself and Mum wasn't around, he'd cry for me. I played with him and showed him things. I did the things that Dad should have done. Now Dad was gone for God knows how long, and it was all official. I'd look after my brother like he was my boy. We'd be okay.

I pulled the keys out of my pocket.

Toby gasped. 'Where did you get those? They're Dad's.'

'Yeah. He doesn't need them at the moment. They don't work on the locks where he is.'

Toby nodded. 'What are you going to do with them?'

I stood up. 'Well, first I think we should let all the birds go free.'

Toby whooped. 'Yeah!'

We unlocked the four big cages and chocked the doors open. The family of rosellas in the last cage seemed to know what was going on. As soon as we'd propped the door with a stick Toby had found, they flashed past. Streaks of red and blue, flying, then gliding in short bursts across the paddock and eventually into the blackwoods along the creek. We left the doors open. We filled up their seed and water. They could come back if they wanted to. The doves in the second aviary fluttered near the door, then flew onto the perches at the back of the cage. Toby wanted to chase them out. I held his hand and said that we should let them decide.

My hands shook and it made the keys rattle as I stood by the door to Dad's shed.

'Come on, Dan, open it up,' Toby said, and pulled at my shorts.

I flicked through the keys and tried a couple before the lock *clinked* open. The pad bolt was heavy and stiff. It eventually opened with a *crack* that echoed off the trees like a gunshot. I shoved the door. We went inside.

Toby screwed up his nose. 'Smells funny in here. Like mice or something. Petrol. Something.'

Dad's shed was as neat as a flower. The tools hung on the walls like they'd grown there. Every one had its place. The spanners for working on the Leyland, the saws and hammers for building things.

Toby picked up a little spirit level.

121

'Don't touch, Toby,' I barked.

He jumped and put it back.

I apologised. I'd sounded like Dad. 'Better leave things as they are.'

He nodded. 'This is spooky, Dan. Can we go now?'

'In a minute, Tobe. You can go if you want. I'll come out in a minute.'

I stood in front of the locked drawer. I could hear my heart beating in my temple like I'd run ten ks. I found the key.

'What are you doing, Dan?' Toby asked.

I slid the key home and the lock jumped open.

'Dan?'

I breathed through my mouth. Short breaths. I pulled the drawer. It slid open freely.

Toby stood next to me and pulled on my shorts. He couldn't see. 'What's in there, Dan?'

Photographs. Kat as a baby. Me as a baby. My first day at kinder. Mum and Dad on a boat. A headstone with flowers. Toby as a newborn, in hospital. Dad with some smiling men. He looked about my age and was smoking a pipe. Dad as a boy. Dad on the beach with some old people who could have been his mum and dad. A Christmas tree. An old car. A ghostly house with windows that looked like the empty eye sockets of a skull.

'Dan?'

Dad as a young man with a girl who didn't look like Mum, fishing from a jetty. Dad with pimples and the same girl. The same girl in a flowing white dress with Dad in a suit and bow tie.

'Dan, what's in there?'

'Nothing much, mate,' I said. Not what I expected. No drugs. No bullets. No rude magazines. I realised that I didn't know my dad at all. Not at all. 'Just some old photos.'

'Can I have a look?'

'Sure,' I said, and handed him a few from the top of the pile. He flicked through without really looking at them. 'Huh,' he said, and handed them back.

'Let's get out of here,' I said.

'Yeah, it stinks, doesn't it, Dan?'

'Uh-huh. It does.'

I left the door unlocked, the drawer unlocked and I unlocked the car and left the keys in the ignition. A dove flew from the aviary, flapping loudly, and landed on the gutter of the house. It was getting dark. It should have been settling down for the night. I thought that it might not survive, that a fox or a cat might eat it. It might not know how to find food.

I sighed. Freedom. It would know freedom.

# twelve

# ECHIDNA

Kat had been suspended. She didn't tell Mum until the following morning when Mum came in to wake her. Kat gave her a note from Mr Grimshaw and Mum closed the door. They talked while I had breakfast. Mum told me that Kat was spending the day with her. I shrugged. I thought about asking if it would be okay to drive my car to Graham and Tina's place. I knew the road like my thumbnail and there was never any traffic at that time of the morning. Mum rubbed her temples. I sighed, kissed her goodbye and jogged to Graham and Tina's place.

Tina asked me about Dad on the way to the bus stop. I told her the truth; that I didn't have a clue why the police had taken him.

'You know,' I said, 'he's lived with me for nearly sixteen years and I don't know him. Is that possible?'

'Sure,' she said. 'That's possible. You can only know someone as much as they want to reveal. Lots of people have secrets.'

'Yeah,' I said. I have mine. My magazines under lock and key. What I think about at night. How I feel when I wake up in the morning. I looked across at Tina and couldn't imagine her having many secrets. Not big ones like Dad has, anyway. She's just too honest and friendly. She doesn't laugh much but she's always happy. Maybe that is her disguise. Maybe she has one smiling face that she gives to me and to the rest of the world, and at home she bites the heads off live chickens.

'I'm really sorry about the mess with your dad, Dan,' she said. 'I hope it all works out okay. If there's anything I can do to help, just yell.'

I thought that the chickens at her place were safe.

Chantelle smiled at me as she bumped down the aisle to the back seat. She waved with the three fingers that weren't holding the strap of her bag. Michael and Amy were in the corner of the back seat, locked in a kiss. When Chantelle sat down they came apart at the lips and started talking. I heard something about lover boy, then Amy shouted, 'Hey, Fairy, how do you spell Chantelle?' and laughed.

The skin on my neck got hot and I looked at the inside of my arm. The scratching had faded a bit but something in me was still red-raw. Amy took great pleasure in salting the wound for me.

'Pooh, something on the bus stinks like wet possum,' Michael yelled. 'Is that you, Fairy? Have you been humping possums again?'

I looked over my shoulder. Amy was laughing. She stopped to stick her middle finger up at me. Michael flashed the gap in his teeth. Chantelle had moved to the corner of the seat and was staring out the window with her arms crossed. Her cheek was red. I thought that she must have got tired of their grade-three games too. She waited until they'd got off the bus before she stood up. She smiled again as she walked past.

'Sorry, Dan,' she mumbled.

I smiled. 'I keep waiting for them to grow up.'

'Yeah,' she said.

I went to Eddy's that night. I strode to the bus to tell Kat, then remembered she'd had the day off. Jake Teychenne stopped me.

'Daniel, isn't it?' he asked.

I nodded.

'Did Kat come to school today?'

'No. She stayed with Mum.'

He looked different and it took me a minute to work out that he wasn't in uniform. He pulled an envelope from his pocket.

'Can you give her this? Will you see her tonight?'

'Yep. Yes, I'll see her and I can give that to her.'

'Cool. Thanks, mate,' he said, as he stuffed the letter into my hand and slapped my shoulder.

Eddy was watering the vegies. She was in her dress and blue and white checked apron, talking to herself. Maybe she was talking to the plants as she sprayed them with the hose. She had her back to me and I didn't want to frighten her so I sang out, 'Hello Eddy.'

'*Ja*, hello Dan-ee-el,' she said without looking. 'Here so soon? Marvellous! Come to work in my garden, good good.'

'Come to pull out that apple tree,' I said, and stopped beside her.

She put her arm over my shoulder and kissed my cheek. 'It's lovely to see you, darling. What is new in your world?'

She had kissed me. She'd kissed me and it felt so natural that my arm slipped around her back and rested there until I realised what I was doing. I pulled my arm away and scratched my head. She smiled.

I looked up the driveway. 'What's new? Nothing much.'

Eddy chuckled. 'You say that but I know that there are many things new, heh, *schat*?'

I shrugged, walked to the shed and grabbed the mattock and shovel.

'Drink, my sweets. Drink,' Eddy whispered to her lettuce as the spray drummed on their leaves. 'Already so dry this year.'

I shook my head and carried the tools to the skeleton of the apple tree.

'What about the bus? The one that broke down near Luke's place? Your new car? Tell me about these things. "Nothing much," he says. *Godverdomme!*'

I pushed on the trunk of the tree. It wasn't going to budge without some serious root pruning. I dug and talked as Eddy watered. Told her about hitting the wallaby in my car. Told her about *Zwarte Piet* the pig.

Eddy laughed and coughed. 'Luke is a beautiful man.

He always brings me vegetables, even though I grow my own. So kind and sweet-hearted.'

'He thinks the same about you.'

'*Ja, ja*. I know. Don't I know!'

I stopped digging.

Eddy smiled at me. 'Come on, work!' she cried, and squirted me with the hose. I jumped and she giggled. A cheeky giggle that made me want to grab the hose and squirt her back. I kept digging.

Eddy sighed. 'Last year he asked me to marry him.'

'He what?'

'*Ja*, marry him.'

'What did you say?'

'I told him I was an old woman. I'm eighty-six for goodness' sake! I have lived on my own for nearly fifteen years. I like to be by my sel-uf. I love him dearly but I have been married. And I don't think that Kasper liked the idea.'

'But Kasper is . . .'

'*Ja*, dead. Dead a long time. His ashes are there,' she said, and squirted an arc over the vegies. I felt a bit sick at the thought of her eating the remains of her husband. Gross.

'Kasper is dead but he still watches over me. That I know.'

I glanced at her.

'When Luke came to ask me to marry him, we had a coffee in the lounge. Drrright in there,' she said, and pointed at the window of the cottage. The sill was lined with blue and white porcelain trinkets.

'Luke would not take no for an answer. I tried to explain to him that I loved him but that I didn't want to be with him all day and all night. He cried and cried.'

She took a breath and bit her lip.

'In my lounge room I have a stand with plants and a collection of shells and little animals made of porcelain and a peacock carved in wood. Luke cried until I had to ask him to leave. He told me that he wasn't going to leave. Not now. Not ever. Me, I got frightened for the first time since my Kasper died. I could do nothing. Nu-thing. And then it happened . . .'

I stopped digging and straightened. She stared at the carrots.

'The stand with the pots began to shake and rattle so,' she said, and held her hand out, palm down and shivering. 'Then mine little porcelain cat leapt off the shelf and landed on the floor. Luke stopped crying and looked at me. All by itself! The plant was shaking, then a shell flew drrright across the room and hit Luke in the chest.'

Sometime during the story, I'd stopped breathing.

'True, *hoor*. Then Luke stood up and like bullets mine little animals shot at him so he had to cover his face. He run for the door and mine wooden peacock spun through the air and crrracked into his head.' She slapped the back of her head and giggled. 'He yelped like a dog and ran outside. Drove home.'

Too much. I shook my head and thumped into an exposed root with the axe end of the mattock. Woodchips spat into the air. One hit me in the chest.

'*Ja*, it doesn't matter if you believe it or not. This is mine

129

experiment. *Hoe ouder, hoe gekker*. The older I get the crazier I become. You will one day have something that you cannot explain and you will know that there is more to life than the things we see and touch. I knew that my Kasper was a spirit trying to help me.'

She wet her fingers and wiped her face. 'At nights I have many times felt him standing by my bed.'

'Ghost?'

'*Ja*, maybe.'

Eddy watered and I dug. It seemed like the normal thing to be talking about the ghost of her dead husband. Kasper the not-so-friendly ghost. As normal as talking about football. For Eddy it was as real as laced leather and the smell of fresh-cut grass. For me, the truth in her eyes sucked me in. Eddy was like all the grandparents I'd never had. Mum's parents had died when I was little. Dad never spoke about his family. When Eddy spoke, I listened with my whole body, my skin prickling and I didn't miss a word. It didn't matter if it was true or just a story.

'Kasper knew he was going to die. He fixed up all his finances. He made our home all like new with new plumbing and a new roof. He booked his trip to Holland and he died on the other side of the world in his home town. He came to me to tell me that he had gone. In my sleep. It was a dream but not really a dream. He woke me like he was going to work, kissed me and said goodbye. I woke and I knew he had gone. I knew with mine whole heart that he had gone. Mine whole heart.'

She sighed and shifted feet. She looked at the sky. 'Ready when you are, Got,' she said.

I stopped digging. I leaned on the mattock and looked at her. 'Careful what you wish for, Eddy.'

'*Ja*, careful. I know what is coming. I am not afraid.'

I opened my mouth to say something, to tell her not to say stuff like that but I couldn't find the words. She packed up the hose and went inside. I thumped into the roots with a new strength. The dirt and woodchips flew.

She came back with a cassette tape. 'Dan-ee-el, I have something to ask of you. A very important thing.'

I rested the mattock against my thigh and dusted my hands.

'When I die . . . maybe it will be years away . . . would you play this music at my funeral? When they burn my body? Please. And take my ashes into the bush. Give them back to the earth.'

She handed me the tape. I opened my mouth to speak and she raised her hand. 'Just say *ja*.'

I didn't really know her. I didn't know about death the way she did. Just a few weeks of working at her home and she wanted me to be at her funeral.

'Eddy . . . I . . .' I said. My brain stalled. The words wouldn't come out. I wanted someone to take me by the ankles, lift me up in the air and shake me like a moneybox so the words would come out. It was all too much. I don't know. Death scares me. Eddy put her hand over mine. Over the cassette.

'It is good to be unsure of death,' she whispered. 'It is what stops you from walking in front of a train or a bus. And I pray that one day you will have an experiment that will show you that death is orright. It's orright.'

131

She let go of my hand and I put the tape in the pocket of my shorts.

'When I was a child . . . nay, not a child, a teenager . . . I had a bad bad disease of the . . . what do you call them?'

She thumped her chest and breathed as though she were choking.

'Lungs?'

'*Ja*! Lerngs. What was it called? Nay, doesn't matter. I am on my back in bed and breathing so,' she said, and laboured another breath. 'Then suddenly I am a spirit and floating on the ceiling, looking down at mine body choking. No pain, *hoor*. I can breathe normal but I am floating near the roof, zooming and diving like from the biggest diving board. Looping around the room.' She held her arms out and pranced around the garden. She stopped.

'Then I am feeling myself being sucked through a big sort of tunnel. So fast through and at the end of the tunnel there is a light so bright, like you have never seen. Never. But it did not hurt mine eyes. Beautiful. I saw mine *groot-moeder* and she hugged me and kissed me so . . .'

Eddy grabbed me and planted a wet kiss on each cheek. I went like a board.

'. . . like she always did when she was alive, but she died when I was seven. I thought to my sel-uf, "But she is dead," and I heard her say, "Do I look dead to you?" Nay. She looked better dead than alive, *hoor*.'

Eddy chuckled. I shifted feet and smiled. Fake smile. Polite smile. Inside I didn't know what to think.

'Then I heard a voice saying, "Nay, it is not your time. You must go back." Kind voice. Gentle. I didn't want to go. If I could have stayed, I would. So beautiful. I would.'

She looked at the top of the dead apple tree. 'When I am staying, that is dying. When I am dying I will be happy. Happy and sad.'

She stared at me. I nodded. I knew what feeling happy-sad was about, though when I thought about Dad I felt more sad than happy. It was like he'd died. The feeling sat heavy in my gut. I leaned on the mattock.

'What is it, *schat*? Are you okay?' she asked.

I almost blurted it out. The words were right there behind my lips. The cops took my dad away. I didn't say it. I opened my mouth but only air came out. A long stop-start sigh. I shook my head. I grabbed the mattock and positioned myself over the root I'd been hacking at.

'You don't have to die just yet, do you?'

She chuckled. 'Nay, I don't know when. Whenever.'

She stepped closer. 'Will you do it for me? Play the music?'

'*Ja*,' I said. *Chop, chop.* Bits of dirt and root went flying.

She smiled and clapped her hands together. 'Good! I'll make a cup of coffee,' she said, and turned to go inside. She paused and broke wind like the air escaping from a balloon stretched at the neck. It rattled on for a few seconds. *Breeeeet.*

She smiled, proudly. 'You didn't know I could play trumpet, hey, *schat*?'

I laughed loudly. I dropped the mattock and put my hand on my knee. I shook my head. 'You're very clever.'

'Thank you, kind man,' she said, and bowed. She shook with quiet laughter as she walked inside.

The next hit with the mattock severed the root. I pushed hard against the trunk and something cracked deep underground. I shoved it again and the dry branches above me rattled. *Crack, crack*. I rocked it back and forth, each time feeling roots pop and tear in the earth beneath my feet. Then the old tree let go and the root-ball sprang out of the ground, peppering my face with dirt. I wiped my eyes and spat. I thought — with a grin — that the best thing about working in people's gardens is the delight that comes from being destructive and making the place look better at the same time. I thought about splitting wood when I got home — the perfect job when you feel like smashing something to pieces.

'Coffee,' Eddy sang, and kicked the back door open. She had two cups and a saucer with two windmill biscuits on it. I hurried over and took a cup from her.

'Here, we'll sit on the seat you've made,' she said, jutting her chin at the trunk of the dead tree. It looked like the perfect seat for two, but as I sat down branches splintered and the seat dropped. I spilled coffee on my leg and jumped. I wiped it off with my dirty hand.

'Is it safe?' Eddy asked.

'Hope so,' I said, as she planted her bottom beside mine. She put the saucer on the ground between us.

She bounced up and down with a smile on her face. '*Ja*, good and strong.'

I sipped my coffee, burning my lip and tongue. My eyes watered. I panted quietly.

'Luke said some kids were teasing you when the bus broke down near his place.'

My shoulders jumped.

Eddy was quiet for a moment. 'Was it the boy who hurt your face? Michael?'

I grunted. 'No, his girlfriend.'

'A girl? It was a girl teasing you? What about?'

I showed her the scratching on the inside of my arm. 'I wrote a girl's name. She said I'd spelt it wrong.'

'Ho? I can't read it without my . . . Chan . . . what does it say?'

'Chantelle.'

'*Ja*? Nice name. Is she a nice girl?'

I shrugged and wriggled. A small branch broke. Eddy and I both sucked in a breath and laughed.

'Is she your girlfriend?' she asked.

'Nah. Just a friend. Maybe not even that. Just someone I like.'

'But you write her name so . . .' she said, and I saw her upturned wrist as she held my arm. It was scarred. Two thick puckered lines of purple-white skin ran from her wrist almost to her elbow.

My mouth hung open and it wasn't just the coffee. 'Um, yeah. I wrote her name. I like her a lot.'

'Does she know that?'

'No. Well, I haven't told her.'

Eddy nodded and sipped her coffee. 'Perhaps you should tell her, Dan-ee-el. *Wie niet waagt, die niet wint.* You don't dare, you don't win.'

I lifted one shoulder. A branch cracked.

'You have only a short time on this earth. Take risks. Not with your life, with your heart. You tell her you like

135

her and what's the worst thing that could happen? *Ja*, she might say, "Nay, I don't like you." Poor thing. But that is life, too, *hoor*. Rejection is part of life too.'

I nodded.

'But what if she says, "*Ja*, Dan-ee-el, I like you too"? Then the love gets bigger and bigger. You are both happier. The world is better.'

I sipped my coffee and looked at my boot. I tried to imagine myself talking to Chantelle like that and nearly choked. I'd rather talk to the plants. I stretched my legs out beside the root-ball. 'What happened to your wrist?'

She twisted her arm and glanced at the scars. 'That happened when I was a teenager. Long time ago.'

She rested her arm against her thigh so I couldn't see the scars. She did it like she was used to hiding them. I thought about what she'd said about taking risks and wondered if it was all rubbish.

'I tried to kill myself.'

I held my breath. A yellow robin dropped out of an apricot tree and landed on the top of my boot. I felt the tiny vibration through my toes. It froze, peering at the soil in the hole.

Eddy nudged me and smiled. 'The nature boy,' she whispered.

With a sharp flutter of wings the bird disappeared into the hole. It flew into the apricot tree again with a beakful of curl grub. I looked at Eddy's wrist.

'During the war I was raped by an American soldier. I felt so dirty. So horrible. So useless. I tried to kill myself.'

'It didn't work?' I asked, and immediately felt the blood colouring my neck and face.

Eddy giggled. 'Nay. My mother found me covered in blood in mine bedroom. She bandaged me on the arm and helped me to a doctor. She kept telling me again and again, "It's not your fault that you were raped. It's not your fault." *Ja*, and it wasn't . . . that man was a monster. I never saw him again. So many times I wanted to find him and kill him. But then the war was over and I forgot about that man. I got married and we shifted to Australia. Kasper and I could never have children. We tried for a long time. Twenty years passed. One day Kasper brought home a friend that he worked with. An American man, a man I'd never met before, but with the same voice as the other man and the same big belly and cigarettes. He came to the farm to visit and I was sitting having a cup of coffee with him when suddenly I wanted to kill him. Tear his eyes out. I had to run outside.'

Eddy's arms swung about like the American was in front of her. Spit flew from her mouth. She slopped her coffee. The tree seat cracked.

'Steady, Eddy,' she said to herself as she wiped the coffee from her apron. 'I stood in the paddock in the rain and asked the heavens, "Why?" and I didn't get an answer. I remembered my mother saying, "It's not your fault." Nay, and it wasn't Kasper's friend's fault either. Some things like that take forever to heal. I forgave that man who raped me then in the paddock. What he did to me was horrible but to hate a man was to invite hate into my life. So I shouted, "I forgive you, I forgive you" with the rain wet in my hair.'

She chuckled. 'Kasper thought I was crazy.'

I shook my head. Some part of me agreed with Kasper. Maybe she was crazy. Just a little bit.

'Kasper was a loving man. Even when I am telling him about when Ziggy was caught in a rabbit trap and about the miracle of him healing, he would smile and say, "*Ja?* That's good darling, amazing. What's for dinner?" Even when we are so close, still he could not believe me. That is when I knew that these things were *mine* experiments. He would have his own.'

She sipped her coffee and nodded her head. 'There is once when he could have died from fright. I almost laughed at him. He would never have forgiven me. We had a toilet outside at the farm. No flush. No light. And at the back of the toilet was a big concrete water tank with no lid. One night I am having a pee and the light comes through the door and I am thinking it is a car coming up the driveway. Oh, we have visitors. But I am looking and the light is coming from behind me. From the water tank.'

Eddy stood up and patted the front of her apron. 'I am wiping so, and I look out. There is a light like the setting sun coming from the tank. So bright and orange.'

She shielded her eyes from the imaginary glare. 'A rolling band of orange fire. It sat there above the water tank and I could see that it was coming from a kind of machine. A UFO. I am not frightened. Not at all. This is not a monster. Friendly. It felt friendly. I went inside to tell Kasper and bring him out to see. He took one look, swore, then dragged me inside. "Quick, under the table," he says to me. "But . . . but . . ." I say, and he is stuffing my head down and closing all the curtains. He crawled under the table with me and he was praying. Never been to church in his life and he was praying. "Dear Mother Mary, Joseph, Jesus, Jesus save us, Got." I had to bite mine tongue so I don't laugh. In the morning, the water tank was almost empty and Kasper didn't want to talk about it. Never a word. He was terrified.'

On the way home that night in Tina's ute, I realised that I didn't have to talk to Eddy about Dad. I knew what she would say. 'Go to him. You must talk with him, *hoor*. Find out what he has done so bad.' And I'd thought, Yeah, could go and see Dad, but I knew I wouldn't. Too easy to find excuses. How would I get there? I'm only a kid; jails aren't good places for kids to hang out. I don't even know where he is.

There was an echidna on the edge of our driveway. It curled into a ball as I walked past and started digging itself into the gravelly soil. I stopped and watched it and thought about going to get Toby. The house was quiet. I thought about it and the strangest thing struck me — Dad was like an echidna. Dad's spikes weren't cream tipped with black and he didn't eat too many ants, but he certainly buried himself in his shed at the first sign of danger. I'd rather hug an echidna.

The house was too quiet. I felt uneasy as I walked to the kitchen door. The car had moved. The P76 wasn't where it had been parked that morning. It was closer to the house. I reached for the handle on the flywire door and it burst open in my face. It was Dad. His jaw was covered in grey stubble. His teeth were bared. He shoved me with both hands and I slammed into the car. Fell to my hands and knees.

'What are you doing going through my stuff?'

He kicked me in the guts. If I had been a football I would have flown fifty metres. I'm not a football. The air rushed from me in a wheeze. Something from my guts was forced into my mouth. Bitter like vomit.

'My friggin' birds . . . you little shit.'

Boot.

'No!' Mum squealed. I looked up and saw that she had him by the hair. She dragged him away from me. He barked in pain and grabbed her arm.

'Stop it!' she shouted. 'Leave him alone.'

Dad belted her across the face with his closed hand. The force of it bounced her off the wall and into the door. She slumped to her knees, held her mouth and sobbed.

Dad panted like a racehorse.

Toby was in the doorway, shaking, with his hands over his ears. Kat came running from her room.

Dad grabbed at the pack on my back. My body tensed. He dragged me away from the car, opened the door and climbed in. The engine cranked but wouldn't start. He stopped and swore, then tried again. The car spluttered to life. The wheels spun and coughed gravel against my leg. I listened without breathing as the car revved down the drive and onto the road. It skidded, then powered into the distance.

It hurt to breathe. I spat at the ground. The bitterness

140

in my mouth was the colour of coffee. Probably was coffee.
I looked up to see Kat's wet face. She held her hand over
her mouth and her whole body sobbed. Tobe still had his
hands over his ears. He looked at me, at Kat, at Mum —
his eyes darting wildly.

'Dan, are you okay?' he shouted.

I nodded and sat up slowly. My guts hurt. My ears were
ringing. There were tears there, bulging behind my eyes.
I drew little breaths and held the tears back. I blinked hard
and looked at Mum. She smiled in defiance and her body
straightened.

'C'mon,' she said with one hand on her cheek and the
other braced against the wall. She stood up. 'Let's get out
of here.'

We camped at Graham and Tina's place that night. Not
far from home but far enough. Mum phoned the police
and they drove out from Milara to interview her. One of
the cops said they were already looking for Dad. They
needed to ask him some more questions.

I wished my life was still as simple as Toby's. He'd
probably seen everything — Dad belting Mum and shov-
ing me around, kicking me — but by the time the last rays
of orange sunlight were highlighting the dust in our
neighbour's lounge room, he was squealing and laughing
and playing with the emu chick. They'd named it 'Chook'
and Toby called its name over and over until Tina put it in
its box.

Tobe drank too much of Tina's homemade lemon
cordial and when he eventually snuggled into the sleeping-
bag on the mattress beside mine, his stomach glugged and

slopped like a hot-water bottle. I hoped he wouldn't wet the bed.

I gave Kat the letter from Jake. I didn't remember it until after I'd crawled into bed and Toby breathed a little-kid-in-sleeping-bliss sigh. I felt Eddy's tape, and the letter was scrunched up with it. I fished them both from the pocket of my shorts and put the tape safely on the hearth near my head. I wriggled close to Kat's mattress. I whispered that I had a letter from Jake. She sat up and snatched it from me.

'When did he . . .? Where did you . . .? Oh God, thank you,' she said, and grabbed me by my pyjama top and kissed me noisily on the cheek. My sister kissed me. Totally, totally gross. Kat got up and went to the toilet. She flicked the light on and stood in the doorway. I wiped my face and smiled as I slipped under my doona. Lucky bitch.

# thirteen

# LIZARD

I could smell smoke when I woke. Pre-dawn gloom. I shook
and fought with my doona. It took a few frantic moments
for me to recognise where I was. The smoke made my
blood race and I scrambled to the door in the half-light.
My stomach grabbed painfully and I cried out.

It wasn't just a hint of smoke; thick and visible clouds
were blowing in on a gusting northerly wind. I couldn't
see any flames, couldn't hear the crackling, but I could taste
it in the air. The phone rang and I jumped. I didn't know
whether to answer it or not.

Tina burst from her bedroom, pulling a silk robe across
her naked shoulders — the breathless panic of someone
who knew a bushfire was devouring the countryside not
far from her home. She didn't see me standing in the
doorway. She didn't see me grab for the doorframe as

waves of feeling nearly knocked me off my feet. The open-mouthed surprise of seeing a naked woman move. An angle of dark hair, the curve and bounce of her body.

'Hello,' she croaked into the receiver. 'Yep, just a minute . . .'

She put the phone on the table and let herself into the spare room where Mum was sleeping. Mum came to the phone in her nightie. Tina slipped back into her bedroom and closed the door.

'Hello?' Mum said, and rubbed her eyes. She winced and looked at her hand. 'Yes . . . um, no. Okay. Thank you for calling.'

Tina burst from the room again, this time clothed except for socks. She turned the lounge-room light on and spoke to Mum.

'Get the kids up. There's a fire.'

Kat was stirring. Tobe's sleeping-bag was dark and wet in the middle. Mum looked at the beds.

'Dan?' she called.

I let go of the doorframe. 'I'm right here.'

'Get dressed quickly. Get Katrina going.'

We piled into the ute. Graham, Tina, Mum and Toby, stinking of piddle, in the front, Kat and me on the back. Tina drove like Graham. Kat's knuckles were white as she held the rail. My side ached on the bumps. If I breathed deeply it felt like someone was spiking me with a nail. I pulled up my shirt and could see a rough circle of blue-black on my ribs about the size of a saucer.

We travelled two kilometres or more and the smoke still billowed and swirled around us. It was no longer the sweet-smelling smoke of a fire in the bush, it stunk like the tip. Plastic, rubber and paint burning. It was hard to breathe. Up ahead I saw the flashing lights of a firetruck parked in the middle of the road. Tina hooted the horn and a fireman jumped and ran to the car. His face and yellow overalls were scribbled with charcoal. Sweat trails had cut lines in the muck and ash on his jaw.

'G'day, Tina,' he said through the window. 'I was just coming down to get you guys. Saved me a trip. Everyone okay?'

'Yes, yes,' Tina said.

I saw Mum through the back window. She touched her face with the tips of her fingers. I could see the shadow of a bruise on her cheek. She was okay.

'Are you all right?' Tina asked.

'Yeah, I'm all right,' he said, and leaned on the door. 'Bit knackered but I'll survive. The worst of it's under control now. There are five units up at Jack's place. They've back-burnt some of the paddocks. If the wind doesn't change, your place will be fine. Can't say the same for the Lanes' house though.'

I heard Tina swear. 'Are Penny and Peta okay?'

'Yeah. They're staying at my place in Henning. We lost their house.'

Tina swore again and signed to Graham.

'What, totalled?' she asked.

'Burnt to the ground. Didn't stand a chance. The fire was lit on the ridge at about two o'clock this morning. When the wind came up it blasted across the creek and into the Lanes' front paddock. They were lucky to get out.

145

Smoke alarm went off inside the house and woke Penny up. Bloody lucky.'

'The fire was lit?'

'Yeah.' The fireman stood up and put his hand on his hip.

'Catch the bastard?'

'Yeah.'

'Thank Christ,' Tina moaned. She signed to Graham. He sat forward and looked at the fireman.

'Anyone we know?' Tina asked.

The fireman grunted. 'Ah, yeah. Could say that.' He rubbed the side of his face. 'We'll be needing a new fire captain.'

'Wha—?'

'None other than the illustrious John Fisher.'


We spent the morning cleaning up on the Lanes' place. I was given a knapsack with a hose attached. The handle on the end of the hose worked like a bike pump and allowed me to spray a jet of water onto any glowing bits of timber or tufts of grass. Graham and Tina had knapsacks too, and we worked our way systematically up the scorched hill. Mum and Kat followed along with big-bladed fire rakes. Toby carried a wet hessian bag. With others from Henning we made sure the place was safe. If the wind changed, no hungry new fires would spring to life.

The wind died down at about midday and word came through on the truck radio that Jack's place had been saved and the fire front had been extinguished. The cheer echoed across the valley.

I was picking my way up an eroded gully, finding tendrils of smoke and spraying them, *sizzle, paf* with my knapsack, pumping the nozzle and making clouds of ash that stung in my nose. I'd almost run out of water when I spotted the wall of a dam. I kicked through blackened grass as I climbed the wall, hoping like anything that the dam would contain enough water to fill my knapsack and save me the long walk back to the firetruck.

The dam did have water in it. I shrugged my knapsack off and saw something floating on the other side. Something dead. I screamed as the memory that had been so tightly locked away in my mind began playing. I couldn't stop it. In the breath of that scream, I saw it all again. The kids hunting skinks amongst the sun-hot rocks. Me and Chris Gemmel. Chris smiling at me, telling me it was time for a swim in the dam. Me agreeing, then spotting a fat stripy skink vanish into a crevice between two football-sized rocks. Chris's gumboots flapping against his bare legs as he ran to the dam. The squeal of delight. The splash. Me rolling the rock aside only to see the stripy tail slink just out of reach. Moving more rocks, and more. Finally holding the cool lizard in my hand and running to show my friend. My friend floating, face-down, hair like weed. The muddy water around him without a ripple. His body still.

I knew I should save him, drag his body from the water, but that boy with the lizard had turned to stone. I couldn't move. I remember thinking that in order to save him I'd have to lose the lizard. Back then the boy couldn't make a sound. I'd stared at the lizard, watching the glossy scales behind its front leg puff and flatten as it breathed.

The stone boy now crumpled. Years later, on the edge of a different dam, the spell was broken. 'Nooooo.'

In my blackened clothes I plowed into the dam. A *whoosh* of spray. I was quickly out of my depth, teeth bared and swimming hard. I grabbed the body and dragged it ashore. Cradled the head with the purple tongue and the ashen eyes. The limp body of a baby goat. I held it to my chest and cried. A mournful wail for the dead. Tears for Chris, for Dad, for my whole mixed-up life.

Tina and Graham ran around the wall of the dam and I cried. Mum and Kat and Tobe arrived beside me and I cried. Mum cradled my head, my sister patted my back, my brother stroked my arm and I cried. Filled up the dam with my tears.

I cried until there was nothing left but aching ribs, a runny nose and shaky sobs. I put the goat kid down and washed my hands and face in the dam. The fire must have panicked it. Probably ran around in the smoke bleating madly until it stumbled into the water. Poor critter.

Someone got a shovel and we buried it beside the dam in funeral quiet. I almost laughed when one of the firemen crossed himself. It was a goat for Godsake!

I told Mum that I'd walk home. She pointed down the hill to where the ute was parked, shrugged and nodded. Toby wanted to come with me and I told him I'd race him back. He could go home via the road and I'd walk through the bush. Kat took his hand and he started dragging her down the hill.

'C'mon, Katty. We're going to win, aren't we?'

Kat chuckled and stumbled behind him.

Mum looked at me for a long time. 'Be careful.'

'Always,' I said, and turned my squelching boots east, down the hill, towards the cool green of the rainforest that bordered the edge of Penny Lane's blackened property.

I sat in the heavy shade of a gnarled old myrtle beech. The canopy above me was alive with scrub wrens and treecreepers. I dug my fingers into the cool humus beside me. I shook my head. Ten minutes' walk up the hill would put me in the middle of a dead black moonscape. Sitting against that huge tree, I could taste the life in the air. I filled my lungs over and over and thought about how symbolic my day had been. It was like a poem about me. Going from a charred place to somewhere green. From old ghosts to sitting in the shade of a tree that may be ten times older than any person who has ever lived. And still growing strong. I felt like someone had taken a fire hose to my insides. It was red and tender in there but it sure was clean. Hope. I felt hope.

My shorts were almost dry. The insides of my pockets were still wet. Eddy's tape! I jumped to my feet and frantically turned my pockets inside out. I remembered I'd left it at Tina's place and let out a rush of air like a punctured tyre. I realised then that I wouldn't let her down. I'd be there at her funeral to play the tape while they burnt her body.

The bracken in the shadow of the big tree was parted by a track. It was pockmarked with the tread pattern of dirt bikes. Yeah, I thought, dirt bikes are one way to get around. I walked.

I found a pocketknife on my way home. Red. Swiss

149

Army. Would have been a great find except there was a name engraved on the biggest blade, 'M Fisher'.

Mum and Kat and Tobe had shifted back home. I could see Toby's sleeping-bag hanging on the clothesline. I found them in the lounge room watching a game show on a crackly black-and-white TV they'd borrowed from Graham and Tina. The phone call that morning, the one that had shaken Tina's house awake, had been the police. They'd found Dad. They were going to keep him until his trial. Mum didn't take her eyes off the telly as she told me and although I heard what she said — that Dad wasn't going to be home that night or any time soon — I still lay awake half the night, listening.

## fourteen

# OWL

I was frightened from sleep in the graveyard dark of early morning by knocking and scratching at my window.

I knew.

I shot from the bed and turned on the light, my heart drumming in my throat. There was nothing at the window.

It had been a dreamless sleep but I knew.

Toby snorted and sighed. Made my skin prickle. I dressed like the house was burning.

I knew without a doubt.

*Knock, scratch, knock* again. I grabbed at the front of my shirt. A feathered face at the window. Curved beak and night-time eyes. An owl. Boobook owl. Its head swivelled to look along the driveway, then it was gone. I held my breath and pulled on my boots. I thought about waking Mum but how would I have explained it? Mum, I just woke up and there was an owl clawing at my window. Yeah, an owl. And now I have to go to Carmine.

Eddy's dead.

# fifteen

# FROG

I was jingling my car keys as I opened the door — shaking like a magpie in a birdbath. I couldn't help it. It took me a minute to find the ignition and another minute to find the switch for the headlights. It was misting rain and I found the switch for the wipers and cleaned the windscreen. It was easy to roll my car down the drive. After that it got hard.

The starter motor whined but the engine wouldn't start. 'Come on,' I said to myself. *Whir, whir, whir.* Nothing. The lights grew dimmer and the engine sounded sicker each time I tried. I turned off the lights and sat there in frustrated silence. I thought about walking home and crawling back into bed, getting out on the right side in a few hours' time and starting the day again.

Eddy.

I put the accelerator to the floor and cranked the key again. The engine coughed, then stopped. Again. Cough, stop.

'Come on.'

Cough, start.

The engine spluttered and popped for half a minute, then purred like the first time it had ever been run. I whooped at the rain-spotted windscreen, then ground the gears as I tried to engage first without the clutch. I was already driving like Graham. What an awesome teacher! I smiled and pressed the clutch to the floor. Select first. Rev, rev, stall.

'Come on,' I cursed. 'Concentrate.'

I started the car again and used more revs. The wheels coughed on the gravel and it stalled. Handbrake off. Try again.

Houston, we have lift-off.

I thought later, as I came to a shuddering halt in front of the mayor's house in Henning, that driving instructors probably have a lower life expectancy than, say, gardeners or park rangers. I'd changed gears successfully, up and down. I hadn't run over anything. I'd stayed mostly on the designated roadway. I'd done all that with my heart racing; breathing like I'd just run the length of the Bellan road. Just sitting next to a learner driver like me could give you a heart attack. I started the car again and indicated left but turned right. Thankfully there were no police doing pre-dawn patrols on the Carmine road.

I hugged the left of the road, occasionally drifting onto the gravel shoulder and correcting so hard that I'd end up over the middle line, panting and swearing to myself, resolving to slow down and take it easy. On a long straight stretch of the Carmine road, near the constellation of lights that is Hepworth A power station, the speedometer read eighty kilometres per hour. I felt like I was flying, with the windscreen wipers thud-thudding the rain away. That's when I saw the lights in the rear-vision mirror and my stomach dropped into the bottom of the bucket seat. Red and blue, flashing. They were some way behind me but I'd already made the decision to pull over and tell them the truth. Maybe they'd come with me to Eddy's and see for themselves. The car chugged to a halt on the shoulder of the road. The lights on the dash shone red. The wipers stuttered. My mouth was dry and I fumbled with the door handle.

The police car sped past. Wailing like a kinder kid with a grazed knee, it seemed to be only fleetingly in contact with the wet road. They were in a hurry but it wasn't to catch me. I rested my head on the steering wheel and panted, mouth open.

The front wheel thudded into the gutter and the car stalled again in front of Eddy's place. I left the keys in the ignition. Rain drummed on the roof. I threw the door shut behind me and it half-closed on part of the seatbelt. A little dog yapped and snarled at next door's fence. I ran along the drive to the front door of the cottage. There was a light on inside. I could hear the TV. My fist hung in the air in front of the door. I didn't want to knock. Inside, someone sneezed. I thumped on the door. The TV went quiet.

'Hello? Who is it?' said Eddy's voice. 'Is there someone there?'

'It's me, Eddy. Daniel.'

'Dan-ee-el. Is that you?' she asked, and I could hear soft footsteps. The porch light flicked on. The door opened a crack and one of Eddy's grey-blue eyes looked through the gap. The door swung open.

'It *is* you! What are you doing here at such an hour in the morning?'

'I . . . I . . .'

'Come in!' she said, and grabbed my hand. She led me into the lounge room.

'Eddy, it's so good to see you,' I said, and hugged her. Her body stiffened and she patted the middle of my back.

She pushed me off to look at my face. 'What is it, *schat*?'

I shrugged. 'I woke up and I thought you were dead.'

'Dead?'

'Yeah. There was an owl at my window.'

'An owl? A bird told you I was dead?'

'Yes. No. Not really. It was a symbol.'

She stared at me for a long time, then her breasts began to heave with silent laughter. 'Do I look dead to you?'

I hung my head. 'No.'

'Nay, I am not dead. Sometimes an owl is just an owl. You came all that way? How did you get here?'

'I drove my car.'

'Oh, *ja*, of course. But you are not old enough.'

'No.'

She took my hand again and slapped my knuckles playfully. 'Naughty boy. You want a cup of coffee?'

I nodded and sat on the leather couch. On the TV

someone was selling a cultured pearl necklace for one hundred and ninety-nine dollars. In the bottom corner of the screen it had the time. Five-oh-seven. I rested my forehead in my hand. I couldn't believe it.

'Next time, *schat*, use the telephone,' she said with a smile as she handed me my cup.

I nodded. There had to be a next time. Eddy would die. When her time came, she'd just go. It was guaranteed. The only thing in life that's guaranteed: death. If something is born, then somewhere along the line it has to die. I looked at the old woman with the half smile on her face and thought that she was my best friend in the world. I wished for my sake that Eddy's death would come later rather than sooner. Much later, so I'd have time to find the words to tell her how I felt. How much I liked being around her. How she had opened my mind with her stories and made me laugh when she broke wind.

Eddy sipped her coffee and put it on the table beside her chair. 'It took courage, Dan-ee-el, to do what you did. To drive all that way. To listen to your feeling. Great courage.'

'Oh, I don't know. Bit stupid really.'

'Nay. Not stupid. Never stupid. What if I had been dead? You would not run away, *hoor*. You would tell someone to get rid of my body. Thank you. I feel honoured.'

I shrugged.

'It is a beautiful thing. You are like an angel in my life. You come to me to make my garden beautiful and you listen to my stories. And not fall asleep!'

157

I thought that it wasn't all one way. Eddy had taught me heaps without trying to teach me anything and she'd got me a great price on my car. I opened my mouth to tell her. I opened my mouth and the words came out.

'Eddy, if I'm honest, I'd have to say that I don't like you.'

Her head rocked into the chair behind her head and she frowned. 'Ho?'

'No. I love you. There's no word in our language between like and love and what I feel in me is much more than like. It must be love.'

She slapped the armrest of her chair and squealed with laughter. She laughed so hard that her dentures leapt from her mouth and clattered into the leg of the coffee table. I lost it. She had one hand over her mouth and the other on her stomach. Her eyes filled with tears.

'Nay. Thtop, thtop,' she gasped. 'No more or I'll pee my panths.'

I laughed harder and she doubled over.

'Nay, too late!' she squealed.

She laughed and no sound came out. Her toothless mouth hung open and the sight of it cracked me up again. I had to sit on the floor for fear of falling there uncontrollably and smashing the table in the process.

Eddy got up from her chair and waddled to the toilet, laughing and coughing. When she returned, she was sighing and wiping her eyes with a fold of toilet tissue. She picked up her dentures and wiped them. They rattled as she slid them into her mouth.

'Had to change my pants,' she grumbled.

I sat in the chair and she held my face with both hands and kissed my cheeks.

'Thank you,' she said. '*Lachen is gezond.* I haven't laughed like that in twenty years. More. Laughter is good. And, my darling, I love you, too.'

Eddy jabbed at the remote for the TV and the picture shrank to a point of light. She moved her coffee and lifted the lid on the table beside her. It was an old record player. She lowered the needle onto an album that was already on the turntable. The speakers popped as the needle landed, then crackled. She sat in her seat and closed her eyes.

'Make yourself comfortable. Listen.'

I leaned back in my chair and closed my eyes. Classical music. Mellow heartbeat bass and soaring violins. It made my eyes water. There were times when my skin crawled. Sometimes the music fluttered like a blown leaf, other times it tumbled like a waterfall and my whole body tingled like my toes and arms and neck were listening.

I sighed when it finished. My body had been swallowed by the couch and I was in no hurry to open my eyes.

Eddy spoke like her words were prayer. 'May the music always cut to our core, chase away the shadows and fill our bones with hope.'

I whispered, 'Amen.'

'Do you have a tape player at home?' Eddy asked.

'No,' I moaned as I stretched.

'Pity.'

'Oh, my sister has. We're not allowed to . . .'

I opened my eyes to find that daylight had begun to

paint the world outside the window in blues and grey. The colours would come with time.

'You're not allowed to what, *schat*?'

I realised that in some part of my mind, Dad was still at home. Force of habit.

'My dad doesn't . . . didn't like music at home. He'd go off at Katrina if she had her music on when he was at home. He's not home anymore.'

'Oh? Why is that?'

'He's in jail.'

She put her hand to her mouth. '*Godverdomme*. What did he do?'

I shrugged and lifted my shirt to show her my bruised side.

'He did that?'

'Yeah.'

'Accident?'

'No.'

'Then he should be in jail. *Wie zijn billen brandt, moet op de blaren zitten*. If you burn your bum, you must sit on the blisters.'

I sat forward and crossed my arms. Eddy didn't even know my dad. That was no great surprise; I didn't know my dad. Sitting in Eddy's lounge room that morning, I *wanted* to know my dad. I wanted to know what he'd done. What had gone wrong? Maybe I did the wrong thing letting his birds go. Maybe I shouldn't have gone into his shed. He'd chucked a wobbly at me so many times before and never hit me. Never kicked me. He hardly ever raised his voice. He didn't have to. I wondered what was worse, a kick in the guts or a week of the grump from hell.

There was a gentle thud on the window beside us. Eddy moved a leaf on the indoor plant and looked at the glass. 'What was that?'

I could see the pale underside and suction-cup feet of a tree frog. It stuck to the glass effortlessly.

'Can you see it?' I asked with a smile.

'Oh! Isn't it beautiful. A froggie!'

She put her hand on mine and looked at me. 'It's trying to tell you something, Dan-ee-el. It is a symbol!'

'Yeah,' I grumbled. 'It's raining.'

She slapped my hand and laughed.

# sixteen
# FISH

I arrived home just as Mum was getting Kat up for school. I saw the light flash on in her bedroom and the curtains opened enough for Mum to see me chugging up the drive.

'Where have you been?' she asked. She was smiling. Maybe she hadn't heard me leave?

'Just down the drive and back. Making sure the car still runs okay.'

She nodded slowly. 'I see. Does it run okay?'

'Yeah. Great. I'm getting the hang of it.'

'Good,' she said. 'You'll have to show me.'

I sighed and whistled as I walked to my room.

I dressed and ate. I was ready to go before Kat. Guilt-powered activity. It had been dumb to drive to Eddy's.

Kat had smiled and laughed her way through breakfast and as we set off to Tina's she started singing.

162

'Do I look all right?' she asked me out of the blue.

She had her hair pulled back; her skin was clean and tanned. She was smiling. 'Yeah. You look good.'

'Ta.'

'Why are you so happy?'

She shrugged and flicked her head so her hair whipped. 'No reason.'

'How are things with Jake?'

She sucked a breath and nodded. 'Yeah, good.'

I kicked a rock and it skittered along the road and stopped a couple of metres in front of Kat. She hopped and skipped, then kicked it back to my side of the road.

'Why did you get suspended?'

'Grimshaw sprung us having a smoke in the bus shelter.'

I looked at her. 'Really?'

'Yeah. Jake reckons he's got a pair of binoculars in the staffroom so he can sniper the smokers.'

I laughed. Kat's a smoker. 'I thought the binoculars were for perving at girls on the oval.'

She grunted. 'Perving at boys, more like.'

Tina was waiting for us on her front verandah. 'Your dad just phoned. He wants you to give him a call, Dan.'

'Piss off,' Kat grumbled. She grabbed my arm. 'Don't, Dan. Let him suffer.'

'Did he say anything else?' I asked.

'Yeah, that he's sorry.'

'Bloody idiot,' Kat snarled.

Tina gave me a piece of paper with the number on it. I stuffed it in my pocket.

'I don't have time to call now,' I said. 'Maybe later.'

Tina shrugged and we bundled into the ute. Kat had stopped singing and her leg jiggled against mine all the way to Henning.

Michael was alone on the back seat of the bus. Amy sat one seat from the back on the opposite side. They stared out their windows. Inside, I was laughing at them. Lover's tiff. Then Chantelle got on. She waved to me and sat behind Amy. I stopped laughing. At least they had lovers to tiff with.

I phoned the Milara Detention Centre from the school payphone at recess. I messed up the number twice and sent the coins rattling into the return bay. Finally a woman answered the phone in a squeaky Barbie-doll voice. It wasn't the sort of voice I associated with prison and I almost laughed. Nervous laugh. My breath had made the receiver wet.

'Hello, I'm trying to get into contact with someone who . . . someone in there . . . my dad. His name's Steven Fairbrother.'

'Hold the line a moment, I'll put you through,' she squeaked, and she was gone. Classical music played while I was on hold. I breathed deeply.

'Hello?'

'Hi, I'm looking for Steven Fairbrother.'

'Speaking. Who's this?'

'It's me, Dad.'

'God, Dan, I didn't recognise your voice. You sound so different. Grown up.'

His voice was almost as squeaky as Barbie's. He was speaking as though his throat was tight.

'Yeah?' I said. I thought about it in the silence and I realised that I'd never spoken to my dad on the phone.

'Sorry, Dan,' he said solemnly.

The phone crackled. How was I supposed to respond to that? It's okay to kick the crap out of me. I shouldn't have gone through your stuff. I deserved it. No way. Nobody deserves to be beaten.

'Apology accepted,' I said.

'How's Mum?'

My mind ticked over in the silence. She's better now you've gone. Happier. She smiles more. 'She's okay.'

'Kat and Tobe?'

'They're all right.'

I could hear someone shouting in the background.

'Sorry, Dan.'

Yeah, you said that already.

'I lost it,' he said.

'Yeah.'

The shouting at the other end died. Dad sniffed. 'Come and visit, Dan. They have visitors and that on Sunday. Visit before they transfer me.'

Yeah, and even if I wanted to, how am I supposed to get there? Walk?

The bell rang.

'I've got to go,' I said.

'Okay, son. Look after yourself.'

Son? That was a new one. 'Yep, see ya,' I said, and hung up the phone. Just before it clunked into its cradle I thought I heard him say something else. I picked it up again and it purred in my ear. I couldn't sit still that afternoon.

Mum had a smile on her face when we got home. She hugged Kat and me. She'd got a lift into town with Graham and done some shopping. The white plastic bags still sat loaded on the kitchen floor.

'Good news,' she said. 'The government is going to pay us money while your dad's . . . while he's not working. Seven hundred . . . nearly eight hundred dollars a fortnight. We'll be okay.'

Toby punched the air with both hands. 'Yesss!'

We laughed.

'More than that though,' Mum continued, and rummaged in her handbag. 'I went to the RTA today.' She pulled out a green plastic card with her picture on it. 'I got my learner's permit.'

'Whooooo!' I shouted, and hugged her around the neck. 'Well done, Mum. Was it hard?'

'Did you get one for me, too?' Kat asked. Her face screwed up as she held Mum's licence.

'No, but I got you this,' Mum said, and handed her a spiral-bound book with a big 'L' and a big 'P' on the front.

'Gee, thanks,' Kat grumbled, and grabbed the book.

The photo of Mum on her licence was beautiful. They're supposed to be ugly, like Dad's. It had made him look . . . well . . . like a criminal. Mum'd taken her hair out and her eyes shone with something. Courage perhaps. Happiness. She looked strong.

After dinner, we set up Tina's TV in the lounge room. Kat brought out her stereo and somehow hooked it up to the television. It was like going to the theatre at home. The four of us huddled on the three-seater couch, and watched a slightly fuzzy *Ace Ventura: Pet Detective*.

Early on Saturday morning a lone motorcycle rumbled past the end of the drive and across the bridge. I knew who it was. Well . . . it looked like Michael's bike. I knew where he was going. Wasn't really that clever a guess — he always went to the shack. I tucked a knife into the pocket of my shorts and started walking.

About a hundred yellow-tailed black cockatoos creaked and squawked like old doors in the pine trees. They can nip a green pine cone to pieces in about five minutes, covering the bed of needles below with their sweet-smelling debris. Pine cones are very hard when they're green. We were banned from using them as grenades at Henning Primary when Mr Nobody threw one and it hit James Sheffield's sister, Corinne, on the shoulder. She squealed for what seemed like an hour. It might have been me who'd thrown it. I picked up the feathered remains of a pine cone from the track and thought that it would take me half an hour with a hammer and chisel to get all the seeds out like the black cockies do.

Michael was nowhere to be seen at the shack. I couldn't hear his bike and the tracks around the entrance were old. I stepped into the gloom and had a poke around. They kept the shack neat. A stack of empty cans reached from the floor beside the fire almost to the corrugated ceiling. I sat in an old car seat that had been propped against the wall and glass tinkled. Behind the seat was a stash of beer —

five small bottles of VB. Before I'd had a chance to think about it, I'd unscrewed the top on one and taken a swig. It bubbled and fizzed as I held it in my mouth. I closed my eyes and swallowed. Some went down the wrong hole and I coughed and spluttered but it tasted okay. It would have been better cold. I drank it anyway.

I could hear a bike in the middle distance. It *rant-rant*ed for a couple of minutes, then cruised up through the gears. Must have made it to the track. I glanced at the beer and shook the bottle from side to side. Three-quarters empty. I sat back in the seat and felt my stomach glow. I was in no hurry to move. Let him come, I thought.

I sat in the gloom and come he did. My heart was trying to leap out of my chest as the shack reverberated and buzzed with the sound. The engine stopped right outside. The spring on the bike stand stretched and twanged. I could hear him grunting quietly as he undid the strap on his helmet. Then he was standing in front of me, blinking and squinting as his eyes adjusted to the gloom.

'G'day, Michael,' I said.

He jumped and his head nearly hit the roof.

'Who's that?' he barked. 'Fairy? What are you doing here? You scared the shit out of me.'

I shrugged. 'Just having a beer. Do you want one?'

He put his fists on his hips. He was breathing hard. 'Yeah, go ahead. Make yourself at friggin' home.'

I held out a bottle. I hoped he wouldn't see my hand shaking in the gloom. He stopped breathing.

'Piss off,' he spat, and kicked dirt at the wall.

'Suit yourself,' I said. I put the bottle down and it

toppled. I stood it up. I felt the knife in my pocket.

'Got something for you,' I said.

He stepped back. 'What?'

I held my hand out.

He didn't move. 'What?'

'Take it.'

He stepped forward and I put the knife in his hand.

'Huh? It's mine. Where did you get that?'

'Found it on a track at the back of the Lanes' place.'

He flicked open the blade and chuckled.

My bottom clenched.

'I reckon I've lost this thing about ten times. Keeps turning up. Thanks.'

He clipped it closed and sat down.

I sighed and handed him a beer.

He screwed the top off and chugged half the bottle, burped and looked at the label on the bottle. 'Bit warm.'

'Yeah, sorry 'bout that. The fridge is busted.'

He grunted. Silence. A gumnut clanked on the roof.

'Should we light a fire?' I asked.

'Piss off. I've had enough fires to cook me a thousand times.'

I laughed, mostly to myself.

'Shut up. It's true!'

'I believe you. And your old man lit them.'

He nodded and drank from his bottle, then forced a burp. 'My old man burns everything. Burns every leaf that falls on the ground. Prunings. When a fox killed all the chooks he burnt the lot of them.'

I screwed up my nose and imagined the smell.

'When our dog, Sadie, died he wouldn't let me bury her. The bastard piled up a heap of logs and burnt her. I bawled my eyes out watching her sizzle and fall to pieces. My dad's sick.'

'Where is he now?' I asked.

'In jail. Where he should be. Friggin' pyro.'

'In Milara?'

'Yeah.'

'With my old man.'

'Bullshit.'

I shook my head.

'What did your old man do?' he asked.

'Dunno.'

'What do you mean?'

'Just that. I dunno what he did.'

'Serious?'

'Yep. Might go and see him tomorrow.'

We finished our beers at the same time.

'Another one, Michael?' I asked.

'Yeah, as long as you stop calling me Michael.'

I sat up. 'You stop calling me Fairy and I'll stop calling you Michael.'

He shrugged. 'Fair enough. Only Mum calls me Michael and then only when she's seriously pissed off at me.'

I handed him a bottle. 'So what do I call you?'

The bottle *fsss*ed. 'Fish. Call me Fish. Everyone else does. What do you want me to call you?'

'Call me Dan. Everyone else doesn't.'

He laughed and held out his bottle. 'Cheers, Dan.'

'Cheers, Fish,' I said, and we clinked bottles.

'Hang on,' he said. 'A toast.' He held his bottle high. 'To the jailbirds.'

I laughed and nearly dropped my bottle. 'To the jailbirds.'

'If you go to Milara tomorrow, I'll come with you.'

'How about, when you go in with your mum, I'll get a lift. My mum doesn't drive yet. I was going to walk.'

'Orright. My mum will do that for us, I reckon.'

We shared the last beer and Fish dinked me on the back of his motorbike right up the drive. Toby bolted from the cubby and jumped up and down when he saw the bike.

Fish set it on the stand and looked at the car. 'I thought you said your mum doesn't drive?'

'She's on her learner's. That's my car.'

He flashed the gap in his teeth at me and wandered to the driver's door. Toby followed.

'Oh, Tobe. This is my . . . mate, Fish. Fish, this is my little brother, Toby.'

'Cool,' Fish said, and held out his hand to Toby.

Tobe took his fingers with his left hand. 'Fish is a funny name,' he said, and Fish laughed.

I grabbed the keys and started the car.

I let Fish drive up and down the driveway a few times with Toby squealing in the back. He was an excellent driver. He said he'd been driving at home since he was ten. I believed him.

'Nice car, Dan,' he said. 'Did well.'

'Now can we have a go on your motorbike, Fishy-wish?' Tobe asked.

'I s'pose. If it's okay with Dan.'

'Yeah. Sit on the front near the tank, Tobe.'

Fish put his helmet on my brother's head but it was too loose to give him much protection. He rode slowly and the helmet muffled Toby's squeals. I thought the boy's face would cramp into a permanent smile. It was still there as Fish and I made arrangements for the morning. Tobe was smiling and waving as the bike fishtailed up the Bellan road. He smiled through tea, laughed through our play fights and rolled into bed with his cheeks pinched. I realised I was smiling, too.

I told Mum that I was going with Fish to see our dads in the morning. She was watching adverts on TV with Kat and she shrugged and looked over her shoulder at me. She stared at me for a long time. There was anger in her eyes; flames that made me want to back off. Made me feel like I'd said the wrong thing.

'Good,' she said through her teeth. 'I won't come.'

'Yeah. I figured that.'

She looked at Kat. 'Do you want to go?'

Kat was shaking her head before Mum had finished asking the question.

'There's a tape on the kitchen table, Dan. Is it yours? Tina found it at her place.'

I picked up the tape and held it to my chest. It was safe.

'Yeah. It's mine,' I said. I had no desire to listen to it. It was sacred. I decided I'd lock it in the cabinet in the cubby.

Mum and Kat's show came back on and they sat forward.

'Is it okay if I drive my car to Henning in the morning?'

'Huh? What? Yes,' she said, and waved for me to be quiet.

I thought I was running late. Dad had locked the shed again and I had to break in to get the jerry full of petrol. I levered the pad bolt straight off the door with a rusty screwdriver I'd found in the cubby. I tipped the whole can into the fuel tank of the Scorpion. Well, most of it. Some splashed on the rear panel. Some splashed on the tyre. It started first try.

I parked in front of the mayor's place and thought that if I didn't know the mayor it would have been a silly place for an unlicensed driver to park. It's not *what* you know that counts, it's *who*.

I grabbed my bag and ran to the bridge. I puffed for a full minute. I couldn't sit on the rail. I couldn't stand still. A silver Land Cruiser flew past. I couldn't remember the sort of car the Fishers owned. Maybe Fish got home and his mum canned the idea. I scuffed a line in the gravel with my boot. Oh well, I thought, can't help bad organisation. I made a promise to myself to go home if the next car that came past wasn't theirs.

I broke my promise. The next car wasn't theirs. It wasn't even a car. It was a big chestnut mare named April and two little dogs named Rabbit and Stacey. Oh, and a rider. A girl in a silly helmet.

My stomach wobbled and I stuffed my hands in the pockets of my shorts.

'Oi! You dogs! Stay away from him, you don't know where he's been,' she said with a smile.

173

'Thanks, Chantelle,' I said. 'I love you, too.'

April was steamed up and snorting. Chantelle slid off the big horse and sat on the rail.

'How are you, Dan?'

I held out my hand and tipped it from side to side.

'Yeah? What are you doing here?'

I sat on the rail beside her. 'Waiting for Fish.'

'Michael Fisher? You're joking . . .'

'Nup.'

'I thought you two hated —'

'Yeah, we did.'

'What happened?'

I shrugged. 'We've got something in common now.'

'What? Did you get a motorbike?'

'Nup.'

'What?'

I looked at her and she smiled.

'Do you have to know everything?' I asked.

'Yeah. I'm a girl. That's my job.'

I grunted.

She pushed me in the arm. 'Come on.'

A car rumbled around the bend in the road. Chantelle led April to the verge beside the bridge. She called the dogs and they scampered from the blackberries and jumped at her hand. Her helmet slid forward and part-covered her eyes.

'It's the Fish-mobile,' she said, and shoved her helmet back. 'What do you guys have in common?'

The car was slowing down. A beaten up old Commodore.

'Our dads,' I said.

They pulled up in the middle of the bridge. You can do that in Henning.

'Your dads?'

Michael was sitting in the front, smiling. I remembered his mum from primary school. She looked older. Her shoulder-length brown hair was wet. She reached over and moved some stuff on the back seat.

'Yeah,' I shouted. 'They live together.'

Chantelle waved to the Fishers. 'But Mr Fisher's in . . .'

I nodded and opened the door. 'See you on the bus tomorrow.'

She smiled. 'You mongrel.'

I chucked my bag on the back seat. Mrs Fisher started driving before I'd closed the door. I waved to Chantelle from the back window. She did a couple of star jumps. Full body waves.

Michael turned to me and his eyebrows jumped. 'Did you really scratch her name into your arm?'

I nodded and looked out the window. Pulled my seat-belt on.

'She's good value,' he said, and looked through the back window. He smiled. 'Oh, Mum, this is Daniel. Dan, this is my mum, Donna.'

'G'day, Mrs Fisher,' I said.

'Donna will do,' she grumbled. 'Are you fellas sure you want to do this?'

Michael looked back at me.

'Yeah,' we chorused.

I said 'Yeah', but I wasn't sure. I could see Fish's leg rocking from side to side.

'Orright,' she said, and turned the radio on flat out. Fish's head started pumping to the music. The speaker behind my head was broken. I was happy about that. My eardrums might have been damaged by the music but at least they wouldn't bleed.

The Milara Detention Centre smelled like sweat. Stale sweat and disinfectant. Not a strong smell but enough to make my nose wrinkle. Donna came into reception and made sure it was okay for us to see our dads. She talked with a short cop through a hole in a Perspex window. She told Fish she'd wait in the car. She kissed him and his face reddened. He hugged her. Another cop came to a side door and unlocked it with a *clank*. He invited us in. I had to leave my bag with the cop behind the counter, and the other bloke led us through some security doors to a room with a desk. There were no windows, only glaring fluorescent tubes behind steel-mesh cages. I could hear my heart beating.

'You guys don't have any weapons or drugs of any kind on you?'

'Nup,' I said.

Fish was quiet. He dug into his pocket and pulled out his Swiss Army knife.

'Got this,' he said, and the cop tutted.

'I'll hang on to that until you get out. Next time, leave it at home. Unless you're hunting or fishing, it's illegal to carry a knife like that.'

'What? Even a Swiss Army?'

The cop nodded.

'That's a bit . . .'

The cop shrugged. 'It's the law.'

Michael's hand shook as he handed the knife over. The policeman put it in a bag and sat it on the desk. 'Which one of you is here to see Mr Fisher?'

Michael put his hand up like he never does in class.

'So, you're young Mr Fairbrother?' he asked me.

'Yep.'

'Right, you're in room three, Mr Fisher. And you're in room one.'

He unlocked another door and led us along a corridor to our rooms. Room one had a small wired-glass window in the door, three chairs, one of those mesh-covered fluorescent lights and a table. I nodded to Fish. He flashed the gap between his teeth and waved with one finger. 'Good luck,' he said.

'Someone will bring your dad up shortly,' the cop said, and closed me in the room.

My toes scrunched in my boots. I stared at a leg of the table for what felt like half an hour. If he gets nasty, I thought, there should be plenty of cops around to give me a hand. I shook my head. Dad wouldn't have a go at me again.

It was a quiet place. Not quiet and alive like the bush but quiet and sort of dead. I tapped my foot on the carpet and the sound pinged off the walls. I wished they'd hurry up, and then I heard them coming along the corridor and I wished I'd never come. There was no air in the room. I breathed deeply and the door swung open.

'There you go, Steve,' said the cop. 'Just yell out when you're done.'

'Thanks,' Dad said, and the door closed behind him.

He smiled. His lips, his cheeks, his eyes were smiling. It wasn't a pretend smile. He wore a blue uniform like the ones he wore to work, only this one had never been covered in coaldust.

'G'day, Dan,' he said. 'Geez I'm sorry, mate.'

I held out my hand. He took it in his paw and pulled me into a hug. I almost squealed. My nose scrunched into his shoulder and he rocked me from side to side. I patted his back and he eventually let me go. We sat on opposite sides of the table. Dad folded his hands on his lap.

'How's your mum?' he asked.

I shrugged. 'Angry.'

He rubbed his chin and nodded. 'That's fair.'

He crossed his arms.

'What happened?' I asked.

'Oh, it's a long story,' he sighed.

'I've got a long time,' I said.

He looked at me. 'Maybe when you're a bit older.'

I clicked my tongue and stood up. 'Right, I'll be off then. I'll come back when I'm a bit older.' I strode to the door and yanked on the handle. It was locked.

'Hang on a minute, mate. Wait on. Sit down.'

The cop came and opened the door. 'Everything all right?'

'Yeah,' Dad said. 'Come on, mate, sit down.'

I sat down and the cop closed the door. Dad sighed and rubbed his chin. I tapped my foot on the carpet.

'One of the guys at work tried to steal a truck.'

I scoffed. 'Stick it in his pocket and walk out the gate?'

'Sort of. Filled it with briquettes and drove it out the side gate.'

This is a joke, right? 'What's that got to do with you?'

'I signed the form to let security know that it was okay. He was going to sell it and give me some of the money. He had a buyer and everything. They were going to ship it off to Perth.'

'It didn't work.'

He leaned back on his chair and crossed his arms. He shook his head. 'The security guard wasn't as dumb as he looked. He phoned the police and they caught Dick driving through Handley.'

Steal a truck? How stupid was that? I could imagine the other guys in jail laughing at him and calling him an amateur.

'Not just any old truck,' he said. 'Brand new Mack. Half a million dollars' worth. I would have been able to retire.'

That was a scary thought; Dad grumping around the house all day, every day. In a way I was glad he'd been caught. Someone laughed in the corridor.

'How long will you get? You won't have to go to jail for long, will you?'

Dad shrugged. 'It's more complicated than it seems.'

'What do you mean?'

He stared at his hands. 'You'll find out . . . when the time's right.'

I stood up.

'Sit down, Dan.'

'Nah, stuff you. I'm sick of your friggin' secrets. I'm off.'

I reached for the door handle and gave it a rattle.

'Dan, stop,' he shouted. 'Sit down. It's stuff you wouldn't understand.'

'What? Try me. What can't I understand? My dad steals a truck so he can retire early. I'm fifteen, Dad. I'm fifteen and I can understand that that was bloody stupid. Come on, try me!'

The cop didn't come.

Dad's mouth opened but his teeth stayed closed as he spoke. 'Stop your bullshit. Sit down. Listen.'

I crunched into the chair and crossed my arms and legs.

'If a word of this leaves this room, I will kill you,' he snarled. 'Do you understand?'

I wiped my mouth on my sleeve. 'Whatever.'

'Do you understand?'

His brow had bunched and his eyes were cold and humourless. It was the old Dad back again.

'Yes,' I said. 'This is between you and me.'

I crossed my fingers in my armpit. And maybe Eddy, I thought, if it's too big to handle. God, what did he do? Maybe I'd hear what he had to say and wish he'd never said it. A secret like that would make me sick.

He put his head in his hands. 'Thank you.'

He took a huge breath and sighed.

'When I was seven there was a bloke who lived down the road from me in Watson. He was a friend of my mum and dad. His name was Barry. Barry was my babysitter.'

He was breathing hard. His hands screwed into fists.

I uncrossed my arms and sat forward.

'Barry did things to me that you wouldn't do to a dog.

Again and again. Mum would drop me off and tell me not to cry. Barry would do . . . he would do what he wanted, then make me so scared that I couldn't tell my mum or dad. I hated my parents for it. I wanted to kill Barry. I wanted to kill him since I was seven years old.'

There was a tear hanging on the side of his nose. His fists were shaking. He sniffed hard.

Sweat tickled down my back. My throat squelched as I swallowed. I wanted him to stop. I could guess the rest of the story and be satisfied.

'I met him in the pub when you were little. He invited me back to his place and I killed him. Drowned him, in his own bath. Drowned him, then turned on an electric heater and threw it in with him to make sure. Sick bastard.'

Dad coughed and his face went red. He pushed his chair away from the table and hung his head between his arms. He spat on the carpet. He wiped his face on his sleeve.

'They fingerprinted me after the truck incident. There's a national register of fingerprints. Mine came up as an exact match with the ones they'd taken from Barry's bathroom.'

He sniffed again.

'So that's why we left Watson.'

He nodded. 'Your mum doesn't even know about that.'

I felt my own rage at Barry. No one deserves to be killed though, I thought. 'And that's why you've been grumpy.'

'Nah, that was years ago,' he said, and flicked his hand at me.

'You've been grumpy for years.'

He chewed on his lip and shrugged.

We fell quiet, like a kettle that has been taken off the boil. Not an uncomfortable silence. It felt like he'd said what he wanted to say.

'Thanks,' I said, and stood up. 'Thanks for telling me straight.'

He stood up and I hugged him. My nose didn't get crushed this time and he sniffed in my ear.

'Thank you. Thanks for coming to see me.'

I nodded.

'Come again? When I find out where I'm going?'

'Yeah,' I said. 'Sometime soon. Got a fair bit of stuff to do at home now.'

Get the phone connected, I thought. Play music loud. Get a proper TV. And a Playstation Two for Toby. Work out a way to tell my old man that he would feel better if he stood in a wet paddock and yelled, 'I forgive you, Barry. I forgive you.'

I grabbed my bag from the cop at the front desk. I almost forgot the parcel. The parcel I'd made for Dad. I took out a big yellow envelope and handed it to the cop.

'I forgot to . . . Can you please give these to my dad?' I said.

He opened the envelope.

'Just photographs and that. I thought he might . . .'

He flicked through the photos from Dad's drawer in the shed. I guessed they wouldn't mean anything to the cop; most of them didn't mean anything to *me*. Every one of them meant something to Dad.

The cop looked at me and smiled a gentle smile. 'Sure. Can do that.'

We didn't talk on the way home. Fish had been crying. Toby scrambled outside as I pulled in the drive, waving with both hands, then wiggling his bare bottom at me. I smiled and tooted.

Mum and Kat dragged me into the lounge room and gave me a full interrogation. I told them about Dad trying to steal the truck. They muffled their laughter with their hands.

'Not a very convincing crook,' Mum said.

I didn't tell them anything else. Dad would tell them in good time. He'd have to. I'd make sure of it. I didn't want any more secrets.

I lit a fire that night. A safe one in the middle of the paddock with the hose standing by. One of the good things about living in Bellan is how isolated it is. Sometimes we do as we please.

I grabbed a cardboard carton from Dad's shed and took it into the cubby. I moved Eddy's tape and filled the box with magazines. They were a secret that I didn't need anymore and the stash became the base for the fire. Toby and I dragged a heap of old timber together, added some more empty boxes from the shed and lit the lot. Toby whooped as the flames licked at the night sky. Mum broke open the liquor cupboard and necked a bottle of port. Tina and Graham drove up in a mild panic about the smoke, then sat and shared Mum's port.

I sat on the grass with my little brother asleep on my knees. I stared at the last of the fire. I turned my face skyward and whispered to the stars, 'I forgive you, Dad. I forgive you.'

# seventeen

# FAIRY

Kat and I played kick-rock with one stone all the way to Tina's. Tina had a headache but wore a smile. She said the port had been a bit rough. We teased her, talking louder than we needed to and mostly about nothing. She told us we could walk.

Fish patted the seat next to him at the back of the bus as I walked up the aisle. Amy sat near him but against the window with her arms crossed.

'Dan, my man,' Fish said, and slapped my leg. 'How are ya?'

'Good, Fish. You?'

'Not bad. Not bad at all.'

I felt like a different sort of fish sitting in silence with them on the back seat. One that was suffering water deficiency. Chantelle sprang onto the bus. Her mouth hung open and she stared at me as she walked along the aisle.

'Shove over, Dan,' she said. 'Let me in.'

She dropped her bag in the aisle and sat next to me.

'His name's not Dan, it's Fairy. Isn't it, Fairy?' Amy said, and uncrossed her arms.

'No. I like Dan.'

'See, told you,' Fish said.

'How do you spell Chantelle, Fairy?' Amy asked.

'C-h-a-n-t-e-l-l-e,' I replied, and held my breath.

'Ha! See, bloody idiot.'

My face grew hot and I shrugged. I thought about moving forward a few seats.

'That's right,' Chantelle said.

The bus lumbered through another gear and we were silent.

'Bullshit. It's S-h-a-n-t-a-l.'

'Nup,' Chantelle said.

Amy crossed her arms. 'Youse don't know how to spell it,' she said, and we all screamed. Well, all of us except Amy, who crossed her arms and looked from under a wrinkled brow at the world dashing past the bus.

I didn't play four square at lunchtime. Chantelle and I sat in the shade of the smokers' tree and I told her the story of my dad. How he'd tried to steal a truck worth half a million dollars and got caught. The bigger reason Dad was in jail sat quietly behind my words. I didn't have to tell her. I didn't have to tell anyone. For Dad and me it wasn't a secret and everyone else who needed to know would find out in time.

Kat and Jake walked across the oval. Well, not really walked; floated. Hand in hand. They sat with us beside the tree and it was easy for me to be happy for her. My sister looked at me with a warm knowing in her eyes and I felt like I wanted to hug her. Get up and dance with her and whoop and scream and laugh.

Fish and Amy smoked and argued behind the tree.

'Isn't love grand?' Chantelle whispered, and nodded at the tree. Her eyes were smiling.

I sighed and shoved her off balance. My whole body was smiling, prickling inside and out with delight. 'Yes. It is.'

She chuckled and sat up.

'Is there a word between *like* and *love*?' I asked.

Chantelle thought about it for a moment, then shook her head. 'Don't think so. What do you mean?'

'Well, I like my car and I like my friends and I like where I live. A lot.'

'Yeah . . .'

'And I like you more than all those things put together. More than *a lot*. More than *heaps*.'

'Okay . . .' she said. Her foot tapped on the grass and she nodded.

'So, Chantelle, I guess . . . I must . . . *love* you.'

She shoved me and I toppled. I lay there smiling. She stood up and brushed the grass from her school dress. She held her hand out to me and her face went the colour of a home-grown jonathan apple.

I took her hand and she pulled me to my feet.

'You've got no idea, Dan.'

'What?'

'You're supposed to hang around and be a pain and after a few weeks ask me if I want to go out with you, and after we've been going out for a couple of weeks, *then* you tell me that you love me.'

'Oh, sorry,' I said. I couldn't tell if she was for real or stirring me up. She was still holding my hand.

She brushed invisible grass off her dress and looked at her runners.

'I've been a pain forever,' I said.

She grunted and nodded.

'So, does that mean I can ask you out?'

She threw my hand down and looked across the oval. 'Hopeless,' she said. She was smiling.

'Hey, Chantelle,' I squeaked.

'What?'

'Will you go out with me?'

She held her chin and tapped a finger on her lips. 'S'pose.'

'Serious?'

'Yeah!'

'Cool,' I said.

'Yeah, cool.'

'I do love you.'

She shoved me and laughed. 'Bonehead.'


I whistled all the way to Eddy's. The sun had lost its sting and she was watering the front garden. At the sight of me she turned the hose off and wiped her hands on her apron.

'Come here, Dan-ee-el. It is so good to see you, *schat*,' she said, kissed my cheek and hugged me. I hugged her like we'd been friends forever. We had coffee and laughed. I told her I'd been to see my dad and she leaned forward. I told her about trying to steal the truck and she scoffed. I told her that Dad had been abused when he was a boy and tears came to her eyes. She held her fingers to her mouth.

'Poor child,' she said.

I told her that Dad was going to jail for killing the man that had abused him. I told her that Dad had said he would kill me if I told anyone, and that I'd wanted to tell her. It was worth the risk. Felt like I had to because we didn't have any secrets and I wanted it to stay that way.

Her head rocked forward and backward slowly. A barely visible nod. She didn't say anything for a long time. She didn't have to.

'Thank you,' she said. 'Thank you for being honest. *Ja*, and I have no need to talk to other people of these things.'

And, I thought, when the time comes for me to keep my promise and play the tape as they burn Eddy's body, those things would burn with her.

'I took your advice,' I said as we hugged goodbye on the footpath at the front of No. 4 Concertina Drive.

'*Jaaaa*?'

'I told Chantelle that I love her.'

'Ho?' she said. She looked at my face. 'And what did she say?'

She took a breath, closed her eyes and crossed her fingers.

'We're going out.'

She jumped and spun and punched the air above her head. Her breasts flipped and swayed under her dress until I thought she was going to knock herself out. 'Yes! Yes! Yes! Good on you!' she shouted.

She grabbed my shoulders and kissed my forehead. 'You are someone to be proud of, Dan-ee-el. You deserve to be happy.'

# eighteen

# MAGPIE

Eddy died one brittle Friday night in August. The seasons had changed. I'd thought she was going to live forever. She died. In her sleep. I didn't feel a thing. She died and I didn't know until Luke phoned. He was one of the first people I'd called when we got our phone connected. I'd called and given him our number, though I never expected he'd have a reason to ring. He told me in husky sobs that she hadn't answered her door when he'd gone to drop off her vegies. He phoned me before he thought about it, he said. He didn't know what else to do. I told him I'd be there as soon as I could. Mum drove my car but she didn't drive fast enough. She'd been driving every day since she got her Ps. She'd dropped Toby at school since he'd started. She'd waited at the bus stop for Kat and me and I'd never noticed how slowly she drove until that Saturday morning. We dropped Toby at Chantelle's place and Chantelle came with us. Mum looked in the rear-vision mirror every few minutes and held the steering wheel as though it might get away if she relaxed. We said nothing.

Near Hepworth B power station, I saw a magpie standing over something dead on the side of the road. Something black and white. With its head tilted, it watched the motionless lump and as we got closer, I could see that the lump was another bird. Another magpie that had been hit by a car. The bird that was alive wasn't looking for a meal, it was mourning. It stood beside the dead bird because it had lost a friend. Maybe a brother or a sister that had shared a nest. Maybe a partner. My heart sank.

Eddy lay in the hollow of her pillow and I wanted to touch her. Shake her gently. Her teeth smiled at us from a glass on the bedside table. She had a look on her face like she'd just snuggled down and sighed. Sighed and died. She wasn't there though. Her body was an empty shell, like her soul had escaped on her last breath. With all the grace of a sunset. I smiled.

I felt sad and happy. Happy and sad. I'd thought that I might have felt her leave. I'd thought maybe an owl might visit again or I'd have some amazing dream or wake up and just know. There was nothing like that. Nothing except I felt like she'd died the way she was meant to. No sirens. No needles and tubes. No watching her fade away. No waiting. It was like I'd walked to her place from school and found that she wasn't home. It felt like she'd stepped into the garden and left her body behind.

I thought all that and then it hit me. I'd never see her

again. The sadness launched itself from the dark part of my soul and crushed the air from my lungs. My beautiful friend. I fell to my knees beside her bed. The old woman who made it seem like my every dream was only a breath away from reality. I grabbed her hand and squeezed the cold fingers, begging her to squeeze back.

'Eddy?'

I felt stranded and lost. Alone in the world. It was a feeling that scorched a path in my mind back to the time when Chris died. I couldn't fill my lungs and couldn't see through the fog of tears. My best friends always die. I closed my eyes and rested my head on the bed. Fitful and noiseless sobs rendered my body useless. The joy leaked from my bones and turned my muscles to mush. What good is an afterlife? Death is death for those of us left in the world. When Eddy's death really hit me, for a moment I wanted to die with her. Just leave.

Mum's hand was hot on my shoulder. I didn't remember it arriving but it must have been there a while. I wiped my face on the bedspread and saw Chantelle. She smiled. It was a sad smile. I wasn't alone. I'd never be alone. Eddy had taught me that. Alone is a state of mind.

'I phoned the funeral directors,' Mum said, sombrely. 'There were two in the Yellow Pages and I phoned the first one listed for Carmine.'

They came and took her body away. A man with a shiny head dressed in a dark suit worked with practised sadness and the efficiency of a waiter at McDonald's. Did we want fries with that open casket? We booked the chapel at the crematorium for Tuesday morning. The man's offsider was a tall man-boy with pimples in his beard. He wasn't that old and I wondered how he'd got into his line of work.

The sky looked depressed that Tuesday. Grey and heavy, like at any moment tears of rain would drown any hope of happiness for the whole day. Kat was immune to it. Jake's parents were going out that night and Jake had arranged to stay at our place. Mum talked with Kat about Jake coming over to stay another night instead and Kat went all weird. She was doing housework and making promises and in the end pleading. Mum agreed to let Jake stay. I told Mum that Kat shouldn't have to stop living because one of my friends had. Mum shrugged and Kat left for Tina's place and the bus with a smile and bounce in her step — half an hour earlier than she needed to.

We dropped Toby at school. I tried to talk him into coming but he wanted to be with his friends. He stood on tiptoes in his gumboots and kissed me through the car window. He told me to have fun.

Chantelle didn't wear black. Not many people at the service did. Chantelle wore her rainbow skivvy and purple skirt. She held my hand in the car and her fingers were cool. There were twenty-two people in the chapel. I recognised Eddy's friends Annika, Claar and Tedi. We exchanged sombre smiles but didn't talk.

Luke stood on his own, staring at the flowers that surrounded Eddy's open coffin. His nose was red and his hair plastered flat with stale-smelling grease.

He shook my hand. 'Hello, Daniel.'

'Luke.'

'It is a sad, sad day to bury such a beautiful person.'

I shrugged and nodded.

'Do you want to say something in the service? I told Daryl that you would want to.'

'Nah . . .' I said, and felt my guts tighten. My only experience of a funeral before that one was the dry-eyed graveside service for my best friend, Chris. I didn't know what to feel then. All the adults around me had cried like kids and I couldn't cry. I didn't cry for Chris until I found that goat in the Lanes' dam. What if I just fell in a heap? I wasn't prepared. What would I say? I stuffed my hand into my pocket and felt the tape. Eddy's tape. Surely the music will say more than a Bible's worth of words.

Luke grabbed my elbow. '*Ja*, you must. You're her son.'

'Nah . . . I'm not her . . .'

He stared at me and nodded.

The man with the shiny head interrupted and asked Luke if we were ready. Luke nodded briskly and sniffed. I handed the tape to the shiny-headed funeral director.

'When would you like me to play it?'

'Oh . . . um . . . when they burn . . .'

'At the committal? Sure. Is it ready to play?'

I nodded.

The man with the shiny head was Daryl and he asked everyone to be seated. I sat in the front row. Luke sat on one side of me, Chantelle on the other. Daryl introduced a religious man who droned on about Edwina and her safe passage into the kingdom of God. He read something with a whole heap of 'thous' and 'thines' that sounded like someone calling a horserace in slow motion. Chantelle squeezed my hand and bit her lip. She wasn't crying. She didn't even look sad. She kind of glowed. Rainbow. Eddy had invited Chantelle and me for dinner in July, and had taught Chantelle how to waltz, the two of them laughing and wheeling round the kitchen while the rice cooked. She'd fed us fat sausages, mashed potato and nasi goreng with a fried banana on top. We'd talked about love, Eddy's favourite topic.

Mum sat beside Chantelle and dabbed at her nose with a blue handkerchief. One of Dad's hankies. Mum had never really met Eddy. Eddy was *my* friend but Mum came to the funeral and cried. I don't think all the tears were for Eddy. And if I lost it and started crying for my dad, or if some of the million tears I'd locked away for Chris leaked out, then no one would really care. Funerals are good like that, I thought.

Daryl raised his eyebrows at Luke and Luke drew a breath and nodded. Head bowed, he moved to stand beside the head of the coffin. His glasses fogged and he honked into a red and white chequered hankie before stuffing it into his jacket pocket. He took some paper from his shirt pocket and unfolded it with shaky hands. His mouth twitched and he cleared his throat. Someone behind me sniffed. Luke glanced at the coffin. His shoulders began to shake. He took a breath and pulled at his tie. His scruffy gold and purple tie. He moved the knot from side to side and I could see the white elastic that held it against his collar.

'I . . . I . . .' he began, and shook his head. For a long while that's all he did. He took his glasses off and rubbed his eyes. Like a yawn, his sadness was contagious. I wanted

195

to put my hand on his back, rub circles and pat like I do for Tobe. Shush in his ear and let him know it would be okay.

He put his glasses back on and tried to read from the paper shaking in his hands. Someone behind me sniffed again and I looked over my shoulder to see Claar, with her long red nails, taking a tissue from Tedi. Then a roar of pain bounced off the walls of the chapel. It made Chantelle flinch and it took me a moment to realise it had been Luke. His face had filled with blood and he screwed his notes into a hard ball and slammed them at the floor.

'I loved dat woman!' he shouted with a spray of spit. He stormed through the gathering and tried to slam one of the heavy chapel doors. It bucked against its springs and settled quietly closed.

A murmur washed through the assembly and faded to a whisper. Chantelle looked at me. Her eyebrows jumped and she poked her bottom lip out. I sighed. I knew I had to do it. Eddy would have liked it. Well, Eddy would have *loved* it. I had to talk. There was nothing heroic about it. It felt like hard work making my body move to the place beside Eddy's coffin. I tried not to look at the body but my eyes had other ideas. They'd put make-up on her and dressed her up for the occasion. The smile still hung on her lips. They'd put her teeth back in but the skin around her eyes had gone slack so she didn't look like Eddy anymore. Eddy had gone, I was sure of that. The spark that ignited the Eddy-fire had gone to another place. Maybe it had just gone out. Maybe it had moved on like Eddy said it would. A prickly heat crawled up my spine. Just in case, I thought, pretend that Eddy's sitting in the corner.

Daryl nodded to me solemnly and his eyes were cold and businesslike. I wondered how many dead bodies he'd seen. I wondered how many funerals he'd stood through. I wondered if he'd buried Chris. I wondered if he had kids and if he could laugh and play-fight with them. I wondered whether pretending to be sad eventually made you sad.

I looked at my mum, her eyes red-rimmed, calm and full of pride. I looked at Chantelle-the-rainbow and she smiled. I looked across the dejected faces and the flower-scented air stuttered into my lungs.

'Sometimes death is a gift. Sometimes it's like the end of a good book. You turn the last page and think, Jeez that was a great story.'

Someone near the back stifled a laugh.

'You don't want it to end. You never want it to end. When a boy dies . . . when a boy drowns it's like the pages have been torn from the book and you feel ripped off. The story doesn't make any sense. It might take ages for you to realise that it was meant to be a short story. A sad story.

'Eddy's death was the perfect end to an amazing story. The story of her life. I guess you're all part of the story, like me. I guess some of you are even feeling the way I do. Bit sad. Bit hollow inside and so, so happy that Eddy was part of my life.

'If Eddy's right and there is an afterlife, you can guarantee she'll be sitting in a fleecy armchair, smiling at us with a cup of coffee and one of those cinnamon bickies. Those bickies are made in heaven so they're probably still warm on her plate.'

197

There was a rumble of laughter and people shifted in their seats.

'Could you think of a more beautiful, peaceful way to die? To just go to sleep and never wake up? Wouldn't surprise me if she'd planned it.

'She taught me so many things. So many things about life. About fear and courage and being yourself and love. She taught me about love. She taught me these things without trying. Every day. She lived every day like it mattered. She loved her animals and she talked to her plants. She wasn't perfect. Who is? I don't think she'd mind me telling you that she could play a mean tune with her bum.'

A woman in the front row squealed and slapped a hand over her smiling mouth. The rest of the chapel rumbled with quiet laughter. I looked at the body in the coffin and I swear it was smiling.

'I hope it's okay to feel a bit happy as well as a bit sad. The book of Eddy had some beautiful moments and a lovely ending. I'll keep it in the library of my heart just in case I need a bit of a laugh or some wisdom.

'For a long time now I've been asking myself, What would Eddy think about this? And I just realised that the Eddy in me will answer like always.'

My throat ached with crying that needed to be let out. I knew if I said another word my voice would squeak and I'd lose it. I nodded to Daryl and he caught the eye of his offsider who bowed his head before quietly closing the lid of the coffin. The music began to play. Eddy's beautiful music. The music she'd played for me when I thought she'd died. Mellow heartbeat bass and soaring violins. Now she *had* died, the words she'd said came flooding back like lyrics. May the music always cut to our core, chase away the shadows and fill our bones with hope.

My eyes started to melt. My body shook and I stood proud in my pain. Something beneath the coffin gave a little *clunk* and it sank slowly into the pedestal. By the time it had vanished from sight some of the people were crying louder than the music, and I desperately needed a hankie.

We went to Tedi's flat and I stood in the sullen little garden with Mum and Chantelle, while a succession of old people offered us plates of sandwiches and congratulated me on my speech. I shook cold hands and thanked them awkwardly. I stuffed myself until I could hardly walk, not wanting to disappoint any of the tray bearers.

Daryl told me that Eddy's ashes would be ready to be picked up the following morning. Not at the crematorium, at their office in Chandler Street. Why was he telling me? Maybe I *had* become her son. Her next of kin. Grandson, maybe. Whatever. Luke had disappeared and no long-lost relatives had come out of the garden for the funeral. She really had been alone. Alone but never lonely. She left behind good memories and friends. All she had left to do in life was die.

I sat in the back seat with Chantelle on the way home. We didn't say much. The sky had darkened and the wipers stammered as they dragged a light mist from the windscreen. It felt like Mum was chauffeuring us and we held hands. Her fingers were like ice to begin with, but by the time we pulled into her driveway they were warm and alive and I didn't want to let go. Not then or ever. Maybe it was a sense of losing someone you love and maybe it's contagious. I'd lost Chris and Eddy, now the thought of losing Chantelle was skulking around in my head. I shook and forced myself to smile. There's enough heartache in the world without dreaming more into existence.

Outside the car, the dogs were going crazy so Chantelle opened the door. Rabbit jumped in and put pawprints on Chantelle's skirt. He jumped across the seat with his tail cutting the air and licked my mouth. I pushed him off and got out of the car. I spat on the gravel and wiped my face on my sleeve. Chantelle laughed and I felt like grabbing her and tickling her until she couldn't breathe. I stepped around the car and she ran off a few paces and smiled. She rubbed at the pawprints on her skirt. She growled at Rabbit but there was too much smile in her voice and the dog wagged his tail harder.

'Do you want to stay at my place tonight?' I asked her. I asked before I'd thought about it and Mum wound down her window.

'I think one friend sleeping over is enough for tonight, Dan. Can you make it another night? I've got to get home,' Mum said, and I remembered that Jake was coming home on the bus with Kat. What was the big hurry?

'You could stay here,' Chantelle said, and my toes curled in my shoes.

Mum looked at me and shrugged.

'Would it be okay with your mum?' I asked.

'Dad. Mum's on night shift so Dad'll be home. I'll give him a call and find out.'

'We'll make it another night. Don't worry about it,' Mum said. 'C'mon, Dan.'

'Nah. It's no trouble. Won't be a sec,' she said. She ran to the front door and kicked her shoes off. Rabbit and Stacey followed her but bolted back to me when she closed the door in their faces.

Mum looked at me and shook her head.

'What?' I asked.

'You kids grow up too quick.'

I shrugged. 'Can't help it.'

'Yeah, well stop it anyway.'

Chantelle ran back outside in her socks. 'Yeah, that's fine with Dad. He said it'll be an early night though, so we can still get up for the bus tomorrow.'

I wanted to scream and jump up and down like Toby does when he's excited. I held it in. It was hard work and some of the joy leaked out of my eyes.

'What is it, Dan? You okay?' Mum whispered.

I nodded. 'My uniform,' I said.

'I'll drop it off — and your bag — when I come in to get Tobe.'

I hugged her through the window and thanked her.

'You sure you're okay?'

I nodded. 'Just smiling so hard inside that it hurts.'

She scruffed the fuzz on my head and kissed me before parping on the horn as she drove off.

The sun came out as Mum left. It made a faint rainbow in the east. Chantelle and I watched it without making a sound. I took her hand and grunted a laugh when I realised she was standing on the wet driveway in just her socks.

'What?' she asked.

I pointed at her feet.

She shrugged.

I could understand that shrug. Some things are more important than others. What was important right then was that we were together. Together and alone. There were pictures in my head, pictures about some of the things we could do together and alone, and my underwear suddenly felt uncomfortable. I was thankful that the pictures weren't on the big screen for the whole world to see. Chantelle looked at me with her eyes part closed. She put her arms around my head and we kissed. All tongue and lips and breath. On and on. Could she feel that? That burning where our bodies met? She broke from the kiss and pulled my hips to her. She moaned into my neck and I knew she could feel it. Maybe she had pictures of her own?

Chantelle snorted like a pig, then shook with a silent laugh. 'God, how embarrassing.'

I looked over my shoulder. Rabbit had mounted Stacey and was humping on her front leg. My face got hot.

Chantelle hid against my neck and continued to laugh. 'Bloody Rabbit. Always got to get a bit of the action.'

The heat between us vanished and left a glowing feeling of closeness. One day, I thought, when the time is right, we'll love each other senseless.

'Mum'll be home soon,' she said. She led me inside and made us both a Milo.

My mum and Chantelle's mum arrived in quick succession. Mrs Morrison had been shopping and had picked up Chantelle's sister from school on her way home. Lauren dragged her bag along the ground and stopped in front of me. She looked a bit crazy. 'Have you been kissing again?' she asked.

Chantelle scoffed. 'Mind your own business, Lauren.'

'I knew it,' she said. She laughed, dropped her bag and ran to Toby. She heaved and lifted my brother onto her hip. He hung on around her neck for a few paces then he wriggled and Lauren dropped him on his feet. He ran and jumped into my arms. I hugged him and he licked my cheek.

'Gross, keep your tongue in your mouth, slobber dog.'

Tobe jiggled and I let him go.

Chantelle's horse thundered to a halt by the gate, whinnied, snorted, then threw her head around.

'Hello, April, you missing out, hey? Something going on?' Chantelle yelled.

Tobe walked to the gate and held out his hand to the horse. April sniffed at him then nibbled his fingers with her lips. Tobe squealed and backed away laughing.

Mum and Mrs Morrison said hello to each other. Mum didn't have my bag. She looked greyer — her hair, her skin.

'I phoned Dad,' Chantelle told her mum. 'I asked if Dan could stay over tonight.'

Mrs Morrison's eyebrows jumped. 'Oh, did you?'

'Nothing concrete,' my mum said. 'They've got school tomorrow.'

Nothing concrete?

'How was today?' Mrs Morrison asked.

Chantelle shrugged. 'All right.'

'What did your dad say?' Mrs Morrison asked with a sigh.

Chantelle nodded. 'He said it was fine . . . if it was okay with you.'

I held my breath. I think Chantelle and Mum did too.

'That's fine. Just don't go . . . stupid.'

Chantelle nodded and jiggled on the spot. I let go of my breath.

Mrs Morrison turned to Mum. 'Sounds like this has been a long time in the planning.'

Mum's lips pulled tight. 'Yeah. I hope they're not . . . I hope they don't cause you any headaches.'

Mrs Morrison shrugged. 'Rick's home tonight. I'm working. Won't bother me!'

Mum grunted and crossed her arms.

Mrs Morrison looked hard at Mum. 'They'll be fine.'

'Give me a call if there are any hassles.'

Lauren was inviting Toby inside. Tobe looked at Mum and she told him they had to get going. Mrs Morrison asked Mum in for a cuppa and Mum shook her head. She looked at her shoe and said she'd have to keep moving. Her lips were still pulled tight and it looked as though she was going to cry. She ripped open the back door of the Scorpion and grabbed my school bag. She wiped her nose on her wrist and handed me my bag.

'Luke phoned,' she said.

I looked at her face. 'Is he all right?'

204

'Yeah. He wanted to talk to you. Did he call here?'

I shrugged and shook my head.

'I gave him the number.'

Mum looked all tangled up behind her eyes. Maybe she couldn't cope with me being at Chantelle's. I put my bag down and hugged her.

She breathed the words in my ear. 'Your dad phoned as well.'

Suddenly all the shakiness about her made sense. He hadn't phoned for months. He'd been transferred to Fulham — nearly two hours away — and I hadn't visited. Hadn't really thought about him. Until then. I felt a wash of guilt and my gut fluttered.

She pulled back and looked into my eyes. 'He got seventeen years.'

Seventeen years? That news was like a fox in the chook pen of my mind. My thoughts flapped about in my head and banged into the wire. Seventeen years was longer than I'd been alive. Toby would be twenty-three when Dad got out. In myself I didn't feel sad and I thought that maybe I should have. I felt sad for Dad. What a waste of a life. Two lives. He was my father — I had no choice in that — but Mum had married him. Mum had chosen to be with him.

'You all right, Mum?' I asked.

'Yeah. Bit of a shock. He'd been a stranger for a long time. I didn't realise how much I didn't know about him.'

I could tell by the beaten look in her eyes that Dad had told her about things. About the things he had to suffer as a boy and the ugly justice he had found for himself. She wasn't angry with Dad anymore. Something had burst.

With that news, she now knew the answer to so many of the questions in our lives. Like why Dad was so angry, why he couldn't be gentle for even one minute, why he struggled to smile. Why he couldn't laugh.

She called my brother over. 'Come home soon,' she said to me.

I nodded and hugged her again.

She bundled Toby into the front seat and tooted as she left.

Chantelle and I helped make tea. I felt at home. Mr Morrison kept patting me on the back. He patted me on the back when I cut the onion, and again when I got all the pasta into the boiling water without splashing a drop. In all the months I'd been going out with his daughter I'd never really called him anything other than Mr Morrison. That night he wanted me to call him Rick. It felt awkward but he pulled a face every time I called him Mr Morrison.

'Just call him Dad,' Lauren said as we dried the dishes. 'We do.'

'Call him Dad?'

'You talking to me?' Rick said, and flicked me on the leg with the tea towel. Without thinking, I flicked him back and it cracked against his hand. He chased me through the lounge room and dragged me onto the carpet in the hallway. He dug his fingers into my ribs.

'Barley, barley!' I panted, and eventually he let me up.

He puffed and smiled. 'Wuss.'

He was a good dad. Maybe even a great dad, but not my dad. Rick might be a good name to call this man.

We watched *Home and Away* and *The Simpsons*.

Chantelle rested her legs on my lap and Lauren sat beside me and talked the whole time.

'Lauren; teeth, toilet, bed,' Rick shouted from the kitchen.

Lauren groaned, but didn't move. Next thing her dad's in the doorway and she's scampering along the hall.

'What are we going to do about sleeping arrangements?'

'Easy,' Chantelle sang. 'Dan can sleep in my bed.'

Rick grunted. 'And where will you sleep?'

'In my bed.'

'I don't think so,' Rick said. 'Wouldn't be much sleeping going on.'

His tone was friendly and innocent but when he crossed his arms, the skin on my head got prickly and hot. My heart was rattling away in my chest like it needed an oil. Maybe I could sleep on the couch? Maybe I could sleep in the shed with Rabbit and Stacey? I know Rabbit's a good kisser . . .

The phone rang. Lauren garbled through a mouthful of toothpaste that she'd get it.

'There are double bunks in Lauren's room,' Rick suggested.

'Get real, Dad, he's not sleeping with Lauren.'

'Well, it's one of the options. Come on, think of some others.'

'Dan,' Lauren sang. 'It's for you.'

I looked at Chantelle. 'Who is it?' she shouted.

'It's Luke Van Den Dribble or something like that.'

Rick smiled. Timing, I thought. They could work out

where I was sleeping and I'd just sleep there. I took the handset from Lauren.

'Hello?'

'Hi, Daniel. Luke here. How are you?'

'Luke! I'm fine. How are you?'

'*Ja*, I'm okay. Your mum said I might catch you there. I . . . I wanted to say sorry for today,' he said. He sounded old and beaten.

'Sorry? There's nothing to be sorry about. You did . . . you did the best you could.'

Silence. I could hear his dog barking in the background. Stinky old Diamond.

'If there's anything I can do,' he said. 'Please. Call. You got my number?'

'Yeah.'

'Okay. I'll let you get back to . . .' he mumbled.

'Nah, no hurry,' I cut in. 'What are you doing tomorrow?'

'Nothing much. Washing. Making some soup if I get time. Maybe.'

'We're going to get Eddy's ashes at lunchtime. Do you want to come?' Chantelle and I decided that it wouldn't be a big walk from school to the funeral director's office. If we took off at lunchtime we'd make it back to catch the bus.

'*Ja*, that I could do.'

He offered to pick us up from school. We organised a time and a place, and before he hung up there was a lightness in his voice again.

Chantelle was smiling. 'It's all arranged,' she said. She

grabbed a sheet and a pillowcase from the linen cupboard and skipped to her room. Rick had dragged the spare mattress in from Lauren's room and dumped it on the floor beside Chantelle's bed. *Right* beside her bed.

'Leave the door open. Please try to get some sleep.'

'Yup,' Chantelle and I chorused.


When Fish saw us getting onto the bus together the following morning, he made lots of *whoo-hoo* noises. Kat hadn't caught the bus. I looked up the Bellan road and wondered how her sleepover had gone.

Fish couldn't believe that I'd stayed the night at Chantelle's place. He asked me what had gone on and I smiled and shrugged. He laughed and coughed and called me a sly prick. He wouldn't have been able to understand how, when you really love someone, sometimes just being with them is enough. You don't have to *do* anything. He wouldn't believe that a boy and a girl who are in love can lie beside each other and talk for three hours in the dark of a winter's night — about Eddy and camping and school and music and dads — and be satisfied just holding hands. Well, holding hands until they are almost frozen, then falling asleep.

He'd know about the wanting. He'd know about that dream of smooth, warm skin against skin. The smells. The taste. The tingling touch. There'd be no mysteries for him. There'd be no mysteries but I wondered if he knew about love. I laughed to myself — Mr Expert on love. How would I know what love felt like for Fish? God, it felt good to me and the four of us on the back seat felt like a sort of club.

The bus stopped to let the Johnson kids on. Amy sat in the corner of the back seat next to Fish and ate some red fruit jelly with a plastic spoon. As I watched her, she gagged and spat a mouthful of the fruit stuff back into the container.

'That's totally off,' she groaned, and slapped the spoon in the cup and tossed it onto the floor.

'What?' Fish asked. 'Mouldy?'

She kicked the container under the seat in front of her and spat on the floor.

'Charming,' I said.

She pointed out the window.

We stood up to get a better look and Fish groaned.

A calf had just been born. Right beside the fence.

'How beautiful,' Chantelle sang, and I had to agree. Death and birth. It made me smile.

As the bus lurched off, I could see the cow licking and chomping at the afterbirth that covered her black-and-white baby. Afterbirth the colour of red fruit jelly.

Had to laugh.

# nineteen

# EAGLE

Luke arrived on time and stayed in the car while Chantelle and I talked with Daryl about the service. He gave me a small ornately carved wooden box, not much bigger than a long-life milk carton. I could hold it in one hand.

'That's it?' I asked.

Daryl chuckled good-naturedly, and nodded. 'Doesn't seem like much, does it?'

I thought about opening the lid. Chantelle pulled on my sleeve. I thanked Daryl and we left.

'That place was freaking me out,' Chantelle said. 'Did you see the side room? Coffins everywhere.'

'Yeah,' I said. Luke's car had a bench seat in the front and we climbed in beside him. 'It's their display room; you know, choose a coffin.' I wondered if they had mannequins in the boxes.

'Where to?' Luke asked, and started the car.

Chantelle looked at me. Her eyes were smiling. She was ready for adventure.

'Bellan,' I said.

'*Ja?*'

Chantelle nodded.

'Okay,' Luke said with a shrug, and drove off.

We were quiet until we reached the outskirts of Carmine. Luke shifted in his seat and sighed. 'Eddy made me the one to look after her will. I went to the solicitor this morning and they read it.'

Chantelle and I looked at the lanky man.

'She left everything to charity; World Wide Fund For Nature, RSPCA, Greenpeace, World Vision. Her house, everything.'

I slapped my thigh and laughed. 'Fantastic.'

'*Ja*, I think so too. Fantastic.'

Even after she's dead, I thought, she's still trying to save the world.

Chantelle looked at me. 'What about Timmy?'

Timmy the cat. The stray that stayed.

'Timmy disappeared,' Luke said. 'I went to feed him the day after Eddy . . . I went to feed him and he was nowhere. I put the food out for him and the next day it was still there. So I asked Mrs Vos down the road and she tells me that he's shifted into her place. Sleeps on the front doormat. Cats are pretty smart.'

Luke's car skidded as he turned onto the dirt Bellan road. It had become potholed and rough as it did every winter and Luke pointed to the 'Summer Traffic Only' sign.

'Sure it's okay down here?'

'Yeah, I live down here.'

'Where are we going?' Chantelle asked.

'You'll see,' I said, but in my heart I was undecided. I'd thought about finding the remains of Eddy's old place, but that is in pine forest now and the pines are too much like a graveyard with their heavy shade and the way the wind whistles through their needles. I wanted to scatter Eddy's ashes somewhere strong and happy.

Luke kept driving, dodging puddles and holding tight to the steering wheel.

'Almost there,' I said as we drove past the remains of Penny Lane's house. The grass had grown with the autumn rains and now her place was the greenest in Bellan. Yes, I thought. Death and birth. 'Just stop near the fence here.'

Luke pulled over but stayed in the car.

I asked him if he wanted to come and he shrugged.

'I'll wait,' he said, and crossed his arms.

I held the barbed wires apart for Chantelle and she did the same for me. I still managed to hook my school pants on the wire and put a small tear in the crotch. We walked up the green hill, then into the forest beside the dam. Down to the little gully and the huge myrtle beech tree that had sheltered me after the fire at Penny's place.

'It's beautiful here,' Chantelle whispered.

A lyrebird called from the other side of the gully, its voice so loud that I felt like covering my ears. Whistling and chortling, pretending it was a rosella, then a kooka-burra, then a shrike-thrush, then a whipbird. Chantelle and I stood frozen, listening. A creaking cockatoo, wren and then chiming like a currawong. Then a sound like sharpening a knife on a stone. It finally stopped singing but we could hear it scratching through the leaf litter.

'This is where fairies live,' Chantelle whispered.

'No,' I whispered. 'They've got a house just up the road.'

She grunted. I held the wooden box up and looked at her. 'How do we do this?' I whispered.

She shrugged. 'Open the lid and tip it out?'

'Do we have to say anything?'

'I dunno.'

I opened the lid. Inside looked like the scrapings from the firebox on the wood heater. Grey and white ash. I put the lid in my pocket, and Chantelle held my hand. I moved to the gnarled roots of the old tree and upturned the container. The ash tumbled out in a cloud and settled on the bark of the roots. It settled on the moss, it settled on the fallen carpet of small gold and green and brown leaves. Some seemed to hang in the air and I realised as I pulled Chantelle closer that it had settled on a tiny but perfect spider's web, giving it form.

'The web of life,' I said.

Chantelle put her hand to her mouth.

'That has to be good medicine.'

The leaves above our heads began to tick with rain. Soon the ash would be washed into the earth, I thought, and Eddy's ashes would become part of the tree. I sighed.

It was over.

The lyrebird sang again. Our uniforms were spotted

214

dark with rain, and crystals of it hung in Chantelle's hair as we walked slowly back to the car.

'One day, when I'm feeling a bit stronger, you'll have to show me where she is,' Luke said.

I handed him the empty container. He looked at it for a moment then slipped it into the glove box. He nodded and bit his bottom lip.

On the way to Chantelle's place I kept filling my lungs and sighing. It was over. On the outside, it had been the hardest time in my life. My dad had gone to jail, my beautiful friend had died, my life had been turned upside down, but on the inside I felt free.

I squeezed Chantelle's hand. She smiled and kissed my cheek.

We stoked the wood heater at Chantelle's place. There was no one else home. We sat beside the fire and said nothing. I stroked her hair and she rested her head on my chest. The flames flickered behind the glass front of the heater and it would have looked like we were watching TV. It was the best movie I'd ever seen.

Mrs Morrison arrived with Lauren and I knew it was time to go. If I was going to catch a ride home with Graham, then I'd have to get to the bus stop. I grabbed my bag. I'd make it if I jogged.

Mrs Morrison said she'd drive me down. I said I'd be right but she insisted. We bundled into the car and rode in silence to the bus stop. Mrs Morrison smiled at me when I kissed her daughter goodbye through the window.

Lauren went psycho. 'She kissed him! Mum, did you see that? He kissed her!'

Chantelle smiled and waved. I felt like I could fly.

Kat stood watching from the bus stop. I didn't see her until she waved to the Morrisons. She had a smile on her face. She was smiling and looking at me. I wanted to hug her. My sister. I wanted to hug her first but I didn't get a chance.

She hugged me. Kissed my cheek.

I hugged her back and we didn't let go.

'Hey, Dan. Haven't seen you for ages.'

'Donkeys, Kat. How'd you go last night?'

She let me go and ran her fingers through her hair. Her face lit up. 'Orright.'

We laughed and sat next to each other in the bus shelter. She had a packet of chips left over from lunch and we shared them.

Apparently, Mum really liked Jake. So did Toby. Jake had slept on my mattress on the floor of Kat's room. Well, he'd *laid* on my mattress. They hadn't slept. Kat giggled and I could see the tired lines under her eyes.

I wanted to hear more. I wanted the whole story. What was being in love like for her? Graham arrived in Tina's ute and the spell was broken.

'Did you hear about Dad?' she asked as she grabbed her bag.

'What?'

'He got seventeen years . . .'

'Yeah, Mum told me.'

'Don't you reckon that's a lot for trying to steal a truck?'

I shrugged. Mum would tell her.

I decided to take my life into my own hands. I needed to feel the cool air on my face. I got Kat to ask Graham if it would be okay to ride in the back of the ute.

He grunted, held his hand out and looked at the sky.

I nodded. I didn't mind getting wet. If it rained, that would be a bonus.

He shrugged and I jumped in.

The wheels spun as he took off up the track and the skin on my face tingled. The wind roared in my ears. My teeth got dry and my lips stuck to them in a smile that came from deep, deep within me. As we pulled into the burnt gully of the Lanes' farm, Graham braked hard. I almost flew over the bonnet.

On the edge of the track sat two wedge-tailed eagles. They'd been tearing at the carcass of a road-kill wallaby. At the sight of us they skipped along the road and unfurled their gigantic wings. Wingtip feathers outstretched like fingers. Graham took his foot off the brake and we coasted underneath them. I felt the air from their wings on my face. I saw the look in their eyes. An all-knowing powerful stare. I stretched my arms. I thanked them. I whooped and the ute took me home.

## MORE BESTSELLING FICTION AVAILABLE FROM PAN MACMILLAN

Scot Gardner
**One Dead Seagull**

*I got a flash of Dad running at me screaming. The brick grabbed and dragged me into the blade. My head smacked into the cover. My arm got stuck at the back of the blade and I could feel it cutting me. Rasping the bone. Red dust. Red blood. Black.*

At times life seems brutal to Wayne. His mum and dad have been best enemies since they broke up, he thinks he loves Mandy but she loves Phillip, and his best mate Den is a serious health hazard. Even if Wayne survives the booby-traps and accidents that face him, Den could still get them both killed!

But no matter what the odds, Wayne has a lot of living to do. He's determined not to rot in the hot sand like a lone dead seagull.

From a fresh new voice comes a serious comedy about what happens when you make a truck-load of mistakes and a handful of gutsy decisions.

'Entertaining and heartfelt . . . Scot Gardner presents pictures of youth with a compassion that endures'
VIEWPOINT

'An often hilarious glimpse into a fifteen-year-old boy's life . . . Gardner has the ability to describe very funny events'
MAGPIES

Scot Gardner
**White Ute Dreaming**

Ernie has a good life. Never has to go to school. Never falls out of love. Never knows what it's like to have his world turned upside down. Ernie's a dog. Unlike Wayne. Wayne is sixteen. Trapped.

With a bite as bad as her bark, his mum could be mistaken for a drill sergeant. With a bottle in a brown paper bag, his dad could be mistaken for a lost cause. But Wayne has found his dream . . . a white ute, Kez, the swag and his yellow dog. To go bush. Live it.

Wayne's best mates move. His favourite uncle dies. His dream takes a hammering. But at the bottom, if you're going to survive, you've got to look up.

From the author of *One Dead Seagull* comes a tragicomedy about life, death and a mad-arsed dog.

'reassuring and real'
VIEWPOINT

'an absorbing, honest and thoughtful novel'
AUSTRALIAN BOOKSELLER & PUBLISHER